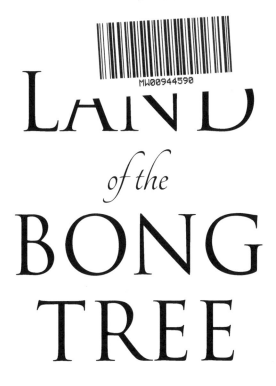

# LAND

## *of the*

# BONG
# TREE

BOOK TWO OF THE *LAND TRILOGY*

P EGGY  G ARDNER

For my children, Morgan and Nick, and my nieces and nephews who have listened to my stories for too many years to count.

# After Jenny's Escape

**Gomer Obadiah Darken:** When the phone rang at 6 a.m. this morning with the news that my stepdaughter, Jenny Hatchet, had shinnied down three stories from Elder Winner's attic, flown the coop so to speak, I longed to whip off my belt, lift her skirts and wallop that shapely ass of hers until she learned the meaning of hellfire.

I have to find her to save myself the disgrace of letting a female under my supervision leave without approval of the Elders. She can outrun the boys in the Compound and might be halfway to Canada or Oregon by now. When I find her and if her mother, Clara—my wife of less than one month—doesn't retaliate so that I have to be succored by my first two wives, I will not spare the rod.

**Maylene Darken:** Sooner or later, I will be suspected of complicity in Jenny's escape, although I was simply an enabler. Josh's mother, Mrs. Barnes, provided the means—the aspidistra plant set in a macramé nest made from forty feet of paracord. The iron-fisted Winner family holding Jenny captive missed that sleight of hand.

Jenny at fifteen with her russet hair billowing out behind her as she runs her 10Ks around the Compound is what I longed to be at her age. Beautiful, innocent, and free of all notions of how things have to be. She taunted my husband Gomer with a cleverness that he couldn't understand.

I was born into my life and have come to terms with it. Jenny has such stamina for being only herself. Her life was in peril. She had to escape.

**Marybeth Darken:** I never seen a man more distraught than my husband Gomer this morning when he got the news that Jenny, an ungrateful hugger-mugger if ever there was one, had spurned the hospitality of the Winner family. As I understand it, she had three square meals, and the Winner sisterwives sat a spell with her every day.

From the minute that Gomer called and said he was bringing a new sisterwife and her two children from Portland to join our family, I knew we was in for a world of hurt. Me and Maylene work like field hands to keep this place going. Our reward was a new sisterwife who has the vapors and two of the sassiest girls that God ever let live.

**Jerry Winner:** My spirits were at low ebb when I had to part with my intended, Abigail Johnson. That pretty little thing was defiant at the end, so it was God's blessing that her neck bent like an arum lily. Sometimes a great sadness tries to settle on me, but I reject it. That feisty, chestnut-haired beauty that Mr. Darken brought back from Portland acted on me like a tonic. God knows when we sink low and lifts us up. Men, that is. Men raise women to joy as they learn to satisfy us. Jenny Hatchet is in need of considerable schooling. Pa's wives were doing their best before she climbed out the window. With no food, water, or money, she won't get far. Our dogs are already tracking her.

**Clara Hatchet Darken:** My darling girl got away! It's been ten hours since the alarm went up and the men shot off in every direction. Gomer says she's probably hiding somewhere in the Compound close to shelter, because she doesn't have skills to last in the forest. I know my Jenny. A girl who could scale down three stories on a thin cord and chew her way through a down comforter will survive—Elder Winner's third wife said Jenny must have cut the comforter in half with her teeth because no kitchen knives were ever on her food tray.

When my husband drove his truck into the Mackenzie River over a year ago, our lives took a wicked twist. I couldn't bear poverty. Gomer promised the moon. He lied. He had promised it twice before—to Maylene and Marybeth, his first two wives and still wed to him by celestial marriage. My child Lorena, who is only seven, has been taken from me to live with the Johnson family to "acclimate." What a harsh punishment. I am pinning my hopes on Jenny and flushing the Valium that Gomer gives me every day.

# CHAPTER 1

## Jenny on the Reservation

In my dream, I am running knee-deep through purple heather on a Yorkshire moor, trying to reach a canvas painting of three misshapen girls with faces similarly ill-defined and a great splotch in the midst of them where their brother had painted himself out of the portrait.

Anne and Charlotte Brontë waltzed out of the painting; Emily stared at me mercilessly, as though shocked that I had somehow betrayed her.

"Heathcliff, get Cathy to sit by Jenny for a while. Hareton, bring me a fresh pan of water. I'll call the clinic if she doesn't wake up soon. She might need an IV. She's very dehydrated and could be delusional—she keeps talking about someone being murdered in a cow pond."

The measured cadence of the woman's voice wasn't alarming; I knew that I had been dreaming about the Brontë sisters. I was freaked out because I awoke to find myself in Wuthering Heights with Emily's characters standing around me. As I struggled to sit up, a vaguely familiar face smiled down at me.

"Are you feeling better, Jenny?"

A trio of faces ranging from pale ecru to copper peered at me as I tried to move my thick tongue to speak. I couldn't make any sense of my surroundings. And then I could. I was on my back in the Belluschi Building of the Portland Art Museum where the Native American art is housed. A woman wearing the Nisga Mask leaned inches away from my face.

The power of speech had left me, but my appreciation for art had not. Shelves of my favorite geometric Pima baskets straddled an alcove with Pomo feather bowls and gleaming black Santa Clara pots. A Tlingit headdress hung above a beaded-handled tomahawk and a ghost shirt decorated with moon and sun designs and little tufts of what might or might not be scalp locks.

My legs refused to move, so I lifted my arms, clasped both hands protectively over my snarly hair and waited for the worst.

"Mother, if you don't give that gruesome Sioux shirt to a museum, I'm going to turn it into a ghost of itself." A young man, probably not much older than me, pointed to the open fireplace that was popping with sparks. "Jenny thinks we're going to scalp her." I was staring up at one of those "chiseled chins" from cheap romance paperbacks, but this one might have been a replica of Apollo, like the armless one at the Portland Museum—except that this flesh and blood version looked familiar and had two functioning arms pulling me into a sitting position. The room spun in a gaudy kaleidoscope of images. Dizzy, I closed my eyes and saw it all happening again.

The fist of Mr. Darken alongside my cheek might have caused the first concussion. When the elders invaded my bedroom, Mr. Darken had shoved a fistful of Quaaludes or Valium down my throat. When I woke up, I was in Elder Winner's attic with his son Jerry panting outside the door like a rutting rhino.

Someone eased me back down on a pillow. I looked up into a trio of faces, motionless, a Nineteenth Century *tableau vivant*, frozen into kind concern. I touched one side of my hair. It was greasy as a slattern's but would stay rooted to my skull. These people were watching over me, not threatening me.

As in one of those old reel-to-reel films, frames doubled back on themselves. I watched my father disappearing into a grave in a Portland cemetery, a for sale sign in our yard, my beautiful, helpless mother stocking shelves in a grocery store, and my sister Lorena reverting to thumb-sucking and bed-wetting as a defense against having to be older than six.

The film stopped as ragged, celluloid fragments hung listlessly. Gomer Obadiah Darken—GOD himself—picked up the ragged ends. Like Attila the Hun rampaging against the Roman Empire, Mr. Darken had besieged our little commonwealth: my mother, Clara Hatchet, widowed only a year, my younger sister Lorena and me, Jenny Hatchet. On my fifteenth birthday, tucked into a new Chrysler with my mother's two-caret diamond, vulgar as a pope's seal, we left our safe lives and shabby apartment.

# CHAPTER 2

During the few weeks I was in the Compound, the sin of lust must have invaded me like the West Nile Virus. Back in my sophomore class in Portland, a few of the nerdy boys were casual friends. I disdained the arrogant jocks. I considered that boys were, in general, obstacles to my goals: first place in the 10K, a full scholarship to a university, and enough money to make the world go around for my mother and sister.

Lately, virus-bearing mosquitoes stung me when I least expected it. There was Josh Barnes with his cerulean eyes pretending not to watch when I flung my leg over a fat horse, exposing whatever was visible through pink, lacy panties filched from my mother's honeymoon stash. On that day in the canyon, we weren't exactly occupied with charging the electric fence, my strategy for getting out of the polygamy Compound.

Now, only a week later as this self-assured, should-have-been-cast in olive marble, gorgeous male knelt beside me, I felt the memory of Josh back in the Compound collapsing with a half-ton punch.

"Are you Josh's girl?" The winsome smile of Hareton followed his unanswerable question.

"Josh?" I croaked out his name as though I were hearing it for the first time.

"Yeah. Our friend. The guy who brought you here last night. Then took off like a scalded cat," he added.

"Let Jenny drink some of this warm broth before you bombard her with questions, Hareton. Heath, put more logs on the fire. She's shivering." The mother of this little circle around me had no name. If I didn't want to end up in the bottom of Dante's Inferno where those who are ungrateful to benefactors go, I'd better show some manners. I could have launched into: to whom am I indebted for cleaning up what I knew was a very nasty creature? Recalling the hours of *vomitus* and trots severe enough to drop an invading army, I was too humiliated to make any reference to my body. I deferred to Josh.

"Josh brought me here?" Somewhere in the muddle of illness, cold, fatigue and a piece of a down comforter that wasn't a substitute for a sleeping bag or toilet paper, I remembered being carried by Josh. I remembered a wet-tongued dog. I remembered thinking that I was dead or should have been. Then I woke up in this warm place surrounded by lovely tawny faces that might have just popped out of a tanning booth.

"Drink some broth, Jenny. You are too dehydrated. We should probably have taken you to our reservation clinic, but that could be risky. We need to keep a low profile. Right now, you're my niece, on my husband's side.

That will explain why you're so pale. You're visiting from Portland."

The beef broth tasted like nectar. My tongue felt only twice its normal size. My headache was subsiding. I could actually feel toes on my right foot. I opened my mouth to insert it: "What do I call my aunt?"

"Izzy. Isabella, but no one calls me that. These are your cousins: Heathcliff, Hareton and Catherine." The grin hardly concealed the family joke that was brewing behind those copper-penny faces. "Last name. What else? Earnshaw."

Broth spewed forth like Mt. Etna bubbling over. My laughter exploded with the raucous, cackling sound of a frightened chicken, but for the first time in weeks, I was no longer afraid. I was Jenny Earnshaw, a paleface from Portland, in a fictional world and safe.

# CHAPTER 3

I awoke in a bed back in the museum, the darkness of it lying heavily about me behind a wall of glass-fronted shelves. Miniature Kachinas stared down at me. I recognized the knobby Mudhead, the Aholi in his blue helmet, and the Crow Mother. My father loved Native American art. He said it represented essential things from long ago when the heavens and the earth and humans were inseparable.

The Crow Mother who whipped girls with a yucca blade at their initiation ceremony was a disturbing idea. At the end of the ceremony, Crow Mother lifted her skirts and whacked herself with the yucca. "She got her just desserts," my father had comforted me as we stood looking at those Kachinas in the Portland Museum, "the way villains always do in Shakespeare and Marlowe plays." The pain of remembering his voice had been unbearable since Mother's fake marriage to Gomer Darken.

A coldness that had nothing to do with the temperature of this bedroom almost stopped my heart. Marybeth Darken probably never saw a Kachina; she most certainly knew nothing about "just desserts" in an Elizabethan drama. She was masterful at whipping young girls.

My so-called stepmother had slashed my little sister's legs with a peach tree switch because Lorena had carried her new kitten into the house. Marybeth was no Crow Mother. She punished the weakest of us because she dare not take on her husband's new wife or me.

I forced myself to sit up; otherwise, I might have drowned in guilty tears of my own making, like Alice in Wonderland. All my plotting to rewire the Compound's electric fence had gone awry. I could still remember the intoxicating splendor of my plan: CPRC elders hanging by their thumbs off the main gate as jagged bolts of electricity sparked like lightning from one hypocrite to the next.

I had envisioned us careening back to Portland—Mother behind the wheel of Mr. Darken's Chrysler with me shouting encouragement and Lorena holding her new kitten in the back seat, sleeping through it all.

Like a failed thief in the night thinking only of my escape, I had rappelled down three stories of the Winner house, slithered under the electric fence in a canyon, swilled down poisonous water and passed out in a forest.

Apparently, Josh Barnes had rescued me. I hadn't managed to save anyone. My mother and sister were at the mercy of those twisted men in the Compound. And, I was in a strange bedroom, alone in my misery.

*Not quite alone.* With a wind-gnawed face that might have been carved from ironwood, an old man sat in the corner of the bedroom on a hard-backed chair, his opaque eyes fixed on me.

I had the odd sensation of being in a bell jar, locked inside, pinned down like a hapless insect. Jenny Earnshaw, nee Hatchet, needed to get herself up and out of this room. Shuffling my feet into moccasins that some big-footed person had left by my bed, I eased myself up and wondered if the old man were as dead as he looked. My experience with the dead was limited: I knew that whatever pieces of my father, James Hatchet, had been rescued from the McKenzie River were inside a fine, gleaming sarcophagus fit for Alexander; at her coffin, I had bent over the stone-cold face of Abigail Johnson in a familiar and loving manner, just so I could check out the state of her neck.

I suppose I could muster enough courage to see if the statue in the corner would respond to a civil comment. "I believe that you may have wandered into my bedroom by accident, sir." There. That was civil.

His head swiveled so quickly that he made the rusty Tin Man look like a gymnast. "I don't do anything by accident. I want to hear with my own ears why Josh Barnes thought he could bring a runaway from the Compound to the Reservation."

Just before we left Portland, I had read *Empire of the Summer Moon*. I knew what Plains Indians did to their captives: beating, raping, scalping, and hacking off noses if the fancy took them. The Northwest Coast Indians were less violent, almost driven to extinction by white men's diseases.

The old man facing me looked as though his constitution could make short work of the pox. So, I gave him the only answer I could: "I don't know why Josh Barnes brought me here. I did run away from those sleazebags. I fully intend to get my mother and sister away from them. If my first plan had worked, you might have seen some of the elders lighting the evening sky." I sunk back on my bed and stared defiantly at him.

"Papa, what are you doing in Jenny's room? I've been looking everywhere for you. Your breakfast is cold." Isabella Earnshaw pushed into the room with a steaming tray.

"Then, I'll eat part of this little runaway's. She won't mind. We've had our talk." He reached across me for the bacon and gave me a smile that must have devastated girls my age fifty years ago.

"The thing is this, Izzy. Three men from the Compound—Darken, Bonner, and Winner—are sitting down in the main office at the gate claiming that Darken's daughter has been kidnapped by Heath with the help of one of their boys, Josh Barnes."

My gasp brought him immediately to the side of my bed. He dropped down, wrapped one long thin arm around me and pilfered the rest of my bacon. "Don't worry, little lady. I happen to know that Gomer Darken doesn't have any children. They can jammer on until the cows come home. We're like monks in one of those medieval monasteries. When someone needs refuge, we provide it."

He pushed himself up with a slight groan. "Damned arthritis. I'll get rid of them, Izzy. We do have a problem though. Someone is leaking information to the Compound. Our business relationships with those people were not my choice. Having Josh's father as our CPA made things mutually beneficial, logging contracts, hauling livestock and the like. Volume got us better deals. In the long run, we should have kept those people at arms length."

He snatched up a piece of toast and winked at me. "I don't think I'll tell them that your niece is visiting from Portland. That could be an issue considering you're an only child, as is your husband. Given that knotty problem, it's best we keep her under wraps for now."

Just as he sauntered through the door, he tossed a zinger at me. "When you feel like talking, I'd like to know just how you were going to light up the sky with those wannabe saints."

"Mrs. Earnshaw." I stuttered as she tucked in the corners of my bed and plumped up my pillow.

"Aunt Izzy, if you remember, Jenny. My father is just being careful. He never trusted those people—except for Josh's family. Josh's father was our tribal CPA for years. Our families are very close. After the death of Mr. Barnes, those elders kept Josh and his mother away from us. Sad. Josh and Heath are best friends."

I flushed as red as a late summer tomato, rotten to the core. Both of those best friends made my heart palpate and my breath quicken. Considering that Heath's mother, my newly acquired aunt, was watching me, I tried to control what was happening in the nether parts of my torso.

"Aunt Izzy, then. I don't want to cause a problem for you or your family. I know what those people do when they don't get their way. They make their own laws."

"Well. We do too, in a way." She patted my cheek. "Tribal law. People from the outside can't come in here and do things without our say-so. However, this place is like any community, lots of decent people and a few low-lifes. The few can cause problems. Papa's right. We'll keep a low profile."

She held out a hand. "Feel like coming into the kitchen? I'll fix us a cup of good coffee. You drink coffee?"

"Love it. Those Compound people don't. I haven't had coffee for a month. Milk with campylobacter or water is the beverage of choice. The caffeine will probably give me a high." I continued to hold her hand. It was a comforting hand, warm and strong.

In oversized moccasins, I shuffled alongside my new aunt into a kitchen that might have made *Architectural Digest*. Gleaming stainless steel subzero refrigerators lined one wall; a huge purple Aga hunkered against the opposite wall. Down the center of the kitchen ran a slab of gray granite with a sink at one end and stools looping the other end. With the exception of that Sioux ghost shirt, the Earnshaw's decorator had remarkable taste.

The scent of fresh coffee almost took me back to that tacky little kitchen in our Portland apartment. Chipped Formica around the sink and vinyl tiles curling at their edges might have been considered Fifties Quaint. In residence since the Cretaceous period, the cockroaches stood their ground against any known deterrents.

Bugs and mice and the homeless were our neighbors. We were safe then. When the scent of freshly ground coffee wafted around me, I blinked back tears. Ground beans plunged through boiling water in a French press was one of our few luxuries. Mother and I took it straight. Lorena drank warmed half and half faintly colored with coffee.

I wiped away my tears with the sleeve of a stranger's nightgown and tried not to think of Lorena being shunted over to the Johnson house so she could learn obedience. I dared not imagine what might be happening to Mother. I just hoped she could continue faking a Valium coma to keep Mr. Darken and Marybeth off guard. Defiance didn't set well with the perverts.

The CPRCers brainwashed dissent out of their kids and cultivated an atmosphere of paranoia about others not of their religion. The Compound was armed against outside heretics.

From a few comments that Jerry Winner had made, I knew he believed that others conspired against his people—even though he was one of the privileged. The sons of elders could choose wives; some of the boys were shunted to distant wards or sent out into the world. For polygamy to thrive, for the older bulls to have their pick of the herd, young males needed to be in short supply.

# Chapter 4

For the next hour, Aunt Izzy and I talked. I told her about my father and our love of Euclid, how we tinkered with the insides of clocks, and how he had trained me to do basic electrical work.

I told her how I planned to electrify the Compound gates. I described Abigail Johnson's bruised neck nestled in the fake satin of her coffin.

Reluctantly, I told her about the perfidy of Mr. Darken. That telling dropped me into a slough of despair. No matter what spin I put on it, Mother came off as simple-minded and an opportunist—who met her match with a conniving bigamist. She was neither. Struggling for words, eyes wide with alarm at the picture I was painting of my mother, I was like an amateur actress in the floodlights who had forgotten her lines. Aunt Izzy supplied them.

"Your mother sounds like a lovely person, Jenny, doing what she thought might help her girls have a better life. Innocent women are the first to fall prey to depraved men like Mr. Darken. His sort learn to . . ."

A loud knock on the back kitchen door startled her. Before she could move to the window to look out, it swung open.

Wearing a big white Stetson with the cockiness of a fop, the tall, thin man made it across the kitchen in two strides and arched his bony form across the counter. The dark circles under his puffy eyes suggested illness or a dissolute life. The knife-like creases in his stiff khaki pants would cut butter.

"It would be a courtesy to wait for a response rather than burst into my kitchen, Ebon. Ebon Riley, Jenny. He's one of the directors of Tribal Enterprises that manage our commercial activities. This is my niece, Jenny Earnshaw."

Mr. Riley eyed me with an absent, unblinking stare as though he might be impervious to my presence; or, there might be nothing brewing behind his fixed expression. He moved around the counter, rolled back on the high heels of polished ostrich-skin boots and stuck out his hand. "Why is it I've never met your niece before, Izzy? Pretty girl like this. Looks to be about fifteen."

"Eighteen, Ebon. She'll be starting college in the fall, majoring in math." Aunt Izzy plotted out my future nicely. I nodded in perfect agreement.

"I'm surprised you've kept her under wraps for so long."

"Family dynamics, Ebon. You should know about that. By the way, how are Eleanor and your son?"

The capillaries from his upper lip to his hairline began working overtime, sending a tidal wave of crimson across his swarthy cheeks. "That b . . ." he ducked his head and sputtered. "She's staying in Spokane. You might want to give her a call when you head back to the university. Try to talk some sense into her. For sake of our boy," he added lamely. Without another word, he spun around, yanked open the door and disappeared.

"Well. That was a charming interlude. So much for keeping a low profile. Not very nice of me to bring up his estranged wife. What he doesn't know is that she's been in touch with me almost every day since she left with her son. I'm helping her find a place near the university in Spokane. She wants to finish her degree. Ebon can't bear independent women."

My newly appointed aunt marched over to the back door and firmly snapped the bolt. "Now I feel like a prisoner in my own house. Ebon is thick as thieves with those men at the Compound. I think he has his own little enterprises on the side with them. Papa is very suspicious of Ebon. He wouldn't have gotten away with it when Josh's father helped manage tribal finances."

"Gotten away with what? I had to come around to the front door. Why is the back door locked? No one locks doors on the Rez," Heath said as he draped himself over the kitchen stool next to me, eyed my coffee, and gulped the remainder.

"Heathcliff, just because I named you after a discourteous gypsy doesn't mean you have to act like you have no manners. Get Jenny another cup of coffee. Papa ate her breakfast, and now you enter the picture."

"Like a Greek bearing gifts," he angled a large plastic sack toward me. "I got Mrs. Masset to open the thrift shop. Cathy's clothes are too small. Hareton's are too ragged and stained. Yours, dear Mother," he kissed her cheek loudly, "are too . . ."

"Matronly?" She purred like a cat ready to spring.

"Never. Too scholarly." He smiled slyly over at me.

"This side of academic robes, which we only wear for graduation, there is no such thing as scholarly clothes. Let's see what rags he's found for you, Jenny."

I pulled out a faded pair of jeans with nicely weathered tears on the legs, a t-shirt from a Red Hot Chili Pepper concert, and a well-worn hoodie with Jimi Hendrix whacking his guitar.

"Perfect, Heath. Just the kind of clothes that suit me. You wouldn't believe what my sister and I had to wear at the Compound. You absolutely wouldn't."

"I would. And the *crème de la crème* is the last of this lot." He held up a pair of Merrill running shoes that looked almost new.

"Mrs. Masset said these came in last week. Size 8. She was saving them for her daughter, but I convinced her that my cousin is a real runner and would be doing barefoot dashes if we couldn't find her some shoes. I told Mrs. Masset that Jenny had to leave her father's house in Portland because he had married a screaming harridan, so she arrived empty handed or should I have said empty footed?"

"You've said quite enough, Heath. Let's not get our stories too convoluted. Mrs. Masset is an old gossip. She repeats everything she hears to anyone who will listen." She pulled aside the blind from the back door window and looked outside. "Ebon Riley just paid an unexpected visit. That's why I locked the back door. He's obviously had contact with those men from the Compound. He came into the kitchen and saw Jenny. His eyes were rolling like a slot machine ready to pay off."

I felt responsible for the tension I was feeling in the room. "I shouldn't stay here." I grabbed the ugly clay ball that still dangled from a leather thong around my neck. Mother had baked her two-caret diamond ring inside of that lump of clay.

"I need help to sell something valuable." I looked into two sets of disbelieving eyes staring at me in my borrowed nightgown. "Then I can get on a bus to Portland."

"And do what?" Heath glared at me as though I had broken the first rule of hospitality.

"Maybe go down the South Coast of Oregon. Mother told me I had an uncle, my father's brother. I never knew that I had one. She only mentioned it as they were putting my father into his grave." I pursed my lips. That sounded really crass, as though my mother might be handing over a pale facsimile of a relative for the man being buried.

"I just don't want to get in the way," I squeaked out, sounding more like my seven-year-old sister than myself.

"We just took you in as a relative, kissing kin so to speak. How could you be in the way? Or think of leaving us?" A slow, delicious smile worked its way up to Heath's umber eyes as he eased an arm around my waist. "The angels come to visit us, and we only know them when they are gone."

Aunt Izzy's sharp smack on her son's shoulder caught his attention. He unwound his arm and plopped down on the stool next to me. "Just funning, Ma."

"If you'd actually read George Eliot instead of just memorizing a few choice quotes, you might have done better on SAT. Your father was counting on Stanford." She dumped beans into the grinder and whacked her fist down with more force than the mechanism needed.

"Oregon, Mother. I'm interested in Northwest Coast archeology, not Peruvian." Heath dusted his hands lightly as though the conversation had just gone into a trash bin.

From the expression on Aunt Izzy's face, it hadn't. She turned what appeared to be a forced smile at me. "We're waffling a bit, Jenny. Getting off the track, but you need to know what we do around here. I work at the university in Spokane most of the week. Nineteenth Century literature. We're on Spring Break, so I'm home this week."

She dumped boiling water into the French Press. "I could take you with me, let you sit in on my classes, but I don't dare take you off the Reservation. I can't put you in school until I think through this situation. Schools require personal information."

Her lips pursed into a thin line. "The elders can't touch you here. You're safe until we can figure out what to do about your mother and sister. My husband is in the field now, so he won't be of any help until he's home."

"Dad is in New Mexico, on a dig. He's a forensic archeologist, looks at diseased bones, arrow holes in skulls, stuff like that. Figures out why people croaked." Hareton's thin voice piped up as though it was still deciding on which register it wanted to use.

"I'll look after Jenny, Mom. I know lots of hiding places."

I ruffled my new cousin's dark hair that poked up stiffly in all directions, like a porcupine's quills. I was very interested in his hiding places. Ebon Riley made me nervous. The description of Mr. Darken's "missing daughter" would perfectly match me.

"You have the rest of this week to spend time with Jenny, if she can stand your company, Hareton. Cathy will be at her friend Stella's most of the week."

Mrs. Earnshaw gave Hareton a quick hug before turning a sober face toward Heath. "If you can remember that politeness is not the same as mauling our guest, Heathcliff, Jenny might like to go down to the stables with you. You were supposed to be finishing off that green mare of mine this week."

While I was imagining a mint-green version of that fat gray mare I rode into the canyon with Josh on a day that seemed long ago, Aunt Izzy handed me my thrift store clothes. Nothing new. Thrift shops in Portland were my stores of choice. In a hushed voice, she pushed a silky wad of bras and panties into my hand.

"A Christmas present from my husband. He still thinks I'm a size 6. I can't bear to disillusion him. Your mother probably wouldn't approve of these things."

Sheer, lacy, leaving nothing to the imagination, the wisps of underwear looked like sea froth on the ocean-green spread in my bedroom. The sturdy, cotton, up-past-the-belly-button "drawers" that Marybeth had given me were off to the trash.

# CHAPTER 5

The first order of business before I visited a green horse was my disgusting body. The last real bath I'd had was in the Winner's claw-footed tub. Fragrant was not a word I'd associate with Leah Winner's soda and water concoction that served as shampoo. The lye soap might be marketed to athletes as "Essence of Gym Socks."

Aunt Izzy was a thoughtful hostess. Not only was the bedside table stacked high with novels, mostly Nineteenth Century, but she had stocked my small bathroom with a new toothbrush, Tom's organic toothpaste, a moisturizer with SP 15, pale lipsticks, eye shadows and liners, and—best of all—enough soaps and shampoos to last through the Apocalypse.

The shirt and jeans were immodestly tight. I examined as much of my backside as I could see in the small mirror above the sink. Even with my loss of a few pounds, the jeans were snug. A gaunt face looked back at me. I cocked my head to examine the purple and yellow bruise from Mr. Darken's fist.

The eyes staring back at me glimmered like those of a yellow tomcat on the prowl, assessing the options, eager to pounce. The old Jenny Hatchet just might be coming back to life. I started down the staircase toward the front room.

"Lord have mercy! Baby's got her blue jeans on." Heath's voice rang out over Van Cliburn playing a Brahms' waltz somewhere in the living room.

"One more rude remark. Just one more, Heathcliff, and Jenny will not have the pleasure of your company today." The threat in Aunt Izzy's voice was decided.

"Blame it on Mel McDaniel, Ma. I'm just repeating what I hear on the radio."

"Quit listening to country music, then. Every time I get into my car, the radio is on 93.7, and the seat is pushed all the way back. I like my Spokane NPR station and not so much legroom if you please. Don't let Jenny get too tired."

Just as we headed out the door, Heath's mother beckoned him back. I could hear them whispering, so I did the decent thing. I strained my ears to hear what they were saying. It had something to do with Mrs. Barnes and a phone.

"So what's going on back at Devil's Den?"

"Mother doesn't want to worry you, Jenny, but it's pointless to keep things from you—when they might concern you." Heath had replaced his usual sardonic expression for a puzzled one. "Mother tried to call Josh's mother. Her phone has been disconnected. When Josh brought you here, he couldn't say much. He had to get back before the men realized he broke the search protocol."

"Protocol?"

"When the Winners found out you'd gone on the lam, the men quickly set up a search grid. They sent Josh over to Highway 95 and told him to check out the Kootenai River. He knew you hadn't gone in that direction. They probably knew it too. The dogs tracked you to the canyon rim. Josh told me he thought you'd take a route that would get you through the fence and hide your tracks from the dogs. That meant you'd follow that creek."

"By accident. It was pitch dark. After I got under the fence in the canyon, I somehow circled back by the cemetery and found an old road. I drank some water. I don't remember much after that." I did, but my dignity wouldn't allow a description of how my body had betrayed me.

"Josh didn't say how he found you. He said he'd be in touch, but he had to take back roads to get to the highway. If they spotted him, he needed to be exactly where they expected him to be. Somebody on the Rez has a bad case of trots of the mouth."

Considering the disgusting state I was in when Josh dumped me on the Earnshaws, I decided to change the conversation. "What color of green?"

"What?"

"Your mother's mare?" I tried to demonstrate interest in her horse, remembering only terror and then relief that the horse Josh had put me aboard showed no rancorous interest in me.

"Oh. Yes. She's green today because St. Patrick's Day is tomorrow. She's a horse of many colors," he said evenly. "Like the one in the Wizard of Oz."

The horse he led out of the barn was black as Satan and just as mean. Her eyes rolled back like marbles in snow, exposing angry white half moons. Heath seemed oblivious to his danger. He talked soothingly and stroked the mare's neck. She repaid him by rearing up and snarling, showing yellow teeth larger than Mr. Darken's.

"You can sit on the top of the corral, Jenny. She's just feeling her oats." Whatever that might mean. Her flashing white-stocking legs disappeared into wickedly sharp hooves, cutting deep trenches as she circled around to avoid being mounted.

In a single, effortless swing, Heath settled into the saddle and moved his right leg back just as the mare twisted its evil muzzle toward the leg in the stirrup, all the time breathing in labored groans. Or, it might have been me doing the loud breathing.

They were moving now, around and around the corral, inextricably bound in their violence—the mare wild-eyed and frantic to dislodge Heath; Heath moved with her lunges as though he might be enjoying this wild ride.

"Open the gate, Jenny. Swing it wide."

I tried pushing and then pulling one end, and moved down to the other to see if a catch might be holding it, when I saw the horse gathering its muscles, the way I do just before the starter gun goes off at a 10K. I shrank back against the corral poles as the horse doubled up and soared over the gate.

It seemed to float in space, its great hunks of muscle moving under sleek black skin. Heath's face lit up like a child's at a circus as the horse landed and galloped past me as though the hounds of hell were on its heels.

"We'd better not tell Mother about that little trick." Hareton's voice searched for a low register, one with more authority. "Heath's supposed to teach that mare to behave, not show off." He reached for my hand. "Why don't I show you the good places?"

The good places included: the loft of a barn with a mountain of hay below that you could jump into—only after you'd checked that no one had left a hay fork in it. Hareton warned me: "Impale you like our ancestors used to snag salmon or gore you like poor Mr. Barnes."

"What do you know about Josh's father, Hareton?" I tried to appear casual, not nosy.

"I know more than I should. At least that's what Mother always says when I get really interesting information. I heard Mom and Dad telling Heath what happened to him. They thought it was too gruesome for Cathy and me to hear. Probably for Cathy. She's only in the fourth grade. I'm in seventh. I know stuff."

"Stuff like what?" I pulled Hareton down by me on a toolbox.

"Stuff like . . . uh . . . Mr. Barnes didn't work around cattle. He liked calculating. Numbers. Math. Like me."

"Me too." I gave him a quick hug and watched a blush flood the face that still had a babyish roundness to it.

"I heard Dad tell Mom that those Compound people moved Mr. Barnes before the county coroner could get there. They cleaned up everything, even the bull that Josh put a pitchfork through. Dad said what they did was purposeful. No crime scene. They even waited most of the day before they called the Sheriff."

A plaintive look settled on his face. "They don't let Josh come here anymore. He might be Heath's *best* friend, but Josh is my friend too. I don't have anyone to help me with math anymore. It's not Mom's strong suit. She likes reading and writing and history—and Dad's in the field half the time."

"What kind of math, Hareton?" I couldn't remember what math I studied in seventh grade. My father and I had been working together on math problems since I could remember—the way other people do crosswords for fun.

"Decimals, fractions, stuff like that. But I know all that. I like geometry and number theory. I don't think Mrs. Houser is too keen on higher math. She says we need to work on practical things, like metric conversion. Boring." He stretched the word out until I wanted to yawn with him.

"Tell you what, Hareton. I'm good at math. I love geometry. I'll help you. Do you know what Euclid did for the . . ." Like a little puppy deprived too long of its water bowl, Hareton lapped up every word. After going through addition and subtraction with Lorena and realizing that she got the I-don't-like-math-gene from Mother, I felt a rush of joy over finding a kindred soul.

"What are you two scheming about?" Heath peered into the barn at us.

"Just stuff." I gave Hareton a high five, and we walked hand in hand out the door.

"Mother's horse is as calm as an old nag. Want to try her, Jenny?"

"Not on your life. I will race you boys to the end of that road over there." I shot off, a pain flashing up my shin, but determined to force my legs back into working order.

Two sullen Earnshaw brothers walked back home with me. Boys can't abide a really fast girl.

# CHAPTER 6

The apparition in white beaded buckskin with enough fringes to decorate the hems of a dozen flappers pasted a trumped up smile on her face and extended three limp fingers toward me. "Sue Ann Snelling. I never knew Heath had a cousin. Charmed."

Like an actress who didn't like the taste of her dialogue, she spun around and clasped Hareton to a chest covered with the armor of beads and flattened quills. "You're getting so handsome, Hareton. I think I should take you to the photo shoot."

"What photo shoot?" Heath shed his muddy boots at the back door, crept soundlessly into the kitchen, and flashed his struggling brother a sympathetic smile.

"For the new tourism brochure. A professional photographer is over at the Casino. He wanted the princess from last year's big powwow. So, I'm obliging." She perched a sort of half-crown, beaded thing atop her head. "Want to go along? Daddy let me have the Benz." She flicked her fingers toward the drive.

Benz. Benzedrine. The kids at my school called them "bennies." I think she meant the red Mercedes convertible in the driveway. Sue Ann's euphoric manner suggested that she was either on something or about to expire under a welter of leather on a warm spring day. Aunt Izzy provided relief.

"Ice water, Sue Ann." She shoved a frosty glass into her hand. "That dress must weigh a ton. You look very attractive," she added without really looking at Sue Ann.

Hareton had distanced himself from the beaded octopus. Heathcliff hadn't responded to her invitation. He looked first at her and then at me before that devilish grin cropped up. "My cousin just got here, Sue Ann. It wouldn't be polite to leave her. I do appreciate the invitation though."

The warning glance he shot his mother was lost in a flurry of fringes and knee-high moccasins stomping out the door as though they had gone on the warpath. "Come again, Sue Ann," Aunt Izzy shouted after the retreating princess.

"Why do you encourage her, Mother?" Heathcliff lifted Sue Ann's untouched water and downed it. "She thinks she's Pocahontas in that get up. I can't stand that tourist trap nonsense."

"Tourism is an important part of our business on the reservation. That big powwow a year ago brought in lots of money to families who need it. Not all the children here grow up as privileged as mine."

"That may be true, but Sue Ann isn't one of them. Her daddy would buy her the moon if she asked for it. He's having trouble buying her a university slot. Sue Ann has never been the studious sort. Goes for instant gratification." There was no mirth in his single guffaw.

"Be that as it may," Aunt Izzy's mouth seamed into a particularly grim line, "you and Josh and Sue Ann used to be good friends when you were kids. You can't forget the importance of friendship."

"If I don't have friends; then I ain't got nothing. Billie Holliday, Ma. Probably when she'd been rescued once again. Speaking of a rescue, I'm worried about Josh. Unless he can get out of the Compound, he's unreachable." Heathcliff looked deadly serious.

"Until he brought Jenny here, I hadn't seen him for over a year, not since his Dad died. He did call every week. Now, the phone's dead. I'm going to take a quick spin over to the Compound, see if I can get past the gate."

I started forward to grab Heath's arm, to shout "No. Don't go there. They might keep you!" when Aunt Izzy shook her head resignedly and pushed me gently back onto a kitchen stool.

"Don't worry, Jenny. Heath isn't in any danger from the CPRC people. He'll just be disappointed again. They won't let him past the gate."

She sank onto a stool next to mine and drank cold coffee absentmindedly. "When Josh's father died, our family tried to go to his funeral. We had been good friends for years. They told us at the gate that it was a private affair. A few days later, Josh and his mother loaded everything they could in the back of the old pickup and left early in the morning." She glanced out the window as though she didn't want to finish the story.

"A deputy picked them up on 93 and escorted them back. We couldn't find out the officer's name or who authorized such a thing. The elders were behind it. They always are. The Barnes were planning to leave the Compound permanently just before the . . . incident."

A gored and trampled CPA hardly qualified as an "incident." At least she didn't say "accident." At the moment, the round, high cheeks that gave her face such a youthful look, dropped like windfall apples. We stared soberly at each other; neither of us had a solution to reclaim those we cared about.

Aunt Izzy's eyes brightened. "You, your mother, and your sister may be just what we need to do something about those people. Kidnapping is a crime in this country. Your mother's marriage to Mr. Darken in Oregon shouldn't complicate things. He's a bigamist. No annulment is necessary. She won't get alimony or anything for all the trouble he's caused."

"A jail sentence would be nice," I muttered.

"I agree, Jenny, but those people own a lot of property in this part of the state. They help fund politicians and, without doubt, some of our so-called county law enforcers. Josh's father told us that the 'temperature' of the place had changed in the past couple of years. He said the elders were stockpiling arms and taking liberties." She frowned. "That's exactly what he said: 'Taking liberties.' I didn't know what that meant at the time."

We both knew what that meant now. Bigamy, kidnapping, and murder. Josh's father and Abigail Johnson. I looked Aunt Izzy steadily in the eye and trusted this woman as I hadn't trusted anyone since my father left me with too many responsibilities. I pulled off my ugly clay pendulum with its sad white daisy.

"Mother got the color wrong, but this is a scarlet pimpernel, and I'm the baron who wears it. I need to use it to save my family." I picked up a large wooden spoon and whacked my mother's pottery creation until it shattered into a dozen shards.

In the center of the debris, a diamond in a heavy gold mounting, sparkled in the late afternoon sun. Aunt Izzy picked it up and turned it speculatively toward the light. "Your mother's?"

"Yes. Third-hand so to speak. Mr. Darken was trying to get it back from her just before the Winners snatched me. She used Mrs. Barnes's kiln on low heat just to dry the clay. I want to sell it and use the money to help Mother and Lorena escape."

"Not on the reservation, dear. There's a pawnshop here that is crooked as a dog's hind leg. I know a respectable jewelry shop in Spokane. I can tell them it's mine and see if I can get a good price for it. Do you want a check? Cash?"

Someone had taken the $80 I'd stashed in my Converse tennis shoes before Maylene brought them to me at the Winner house. I suspected Marybeth. She was a nosy, poke-in-corners kind of person. Cash was not a good idea.

"I'd rather have a bank account and a card to get cash if I need it."

"We can manage that. It will have to be in my name if you trust me. What pin number do you want?"

"It should be 6666, same as the code on the gate to the Compound," I said with a little shiver of pleasure that I might somehow get the best of Mr. Darken.

"What a delicious little intrigue!" Aunt Izzy's face lit up. "This feels like a Dickens' novel with the plot full of twists and turns."

The file cabinets in my brain were popping open and slamming closed as I tried to find a link. The orphan Pip being supported in fine style by a criminal? Or Esther, deserted by her mother, her chances ruined by smallpox, and saved by an older man?

"Don't mind me, Jenny. I'm always trying to make the Nineteenth Century relevant to my students. They can hardly tear themselves away from cell phones and the computer to actually read long novels. They're right there on the Internet: plot, structure, characters, symbolism, and sometimes an actual quote from the author."

She gave me the kind of squeeze she often gave Hareton, brisk and firm. "It's a couple of hours until dinner. There's an iMac in my office just down the hall. You're free to use it. We have a good broadband system on the reservation. I've declared a moratorium on my use during Spring Break. I'm only reading from paper."

This reservation with an affectionate family that had taken me under its collective wing—now offered Internet access. The old hags on Olympus spinning out my fate may have taken a coffee break. I trotted down the hall toward information central. Somewhere on the Oregon coast, I might find a missing uncle.

# CHAPTER 7

After an hour of searching white pages, yellow pages, and anything remotely connected to the name Hatchet on the coast of Oregon, I came up with the phone numbers of two women and an unappealing ad for a fishing charter boat in Charleston with the unlikely name of "Hal's Holiday."

If my father James and his brother had been so estranged from each other that they hadn't spoken in years, I had to ask myself why my uncle would want to hear from a niece he probably didn't know existed. Bringing news that his only brother was dead? And his sister-in-law and another niece held captive in a polygamist concentration camp?

It was time to run. To clear my thinking. My new running shoes were a half size too large, but they were marvelously comfortable. I shot past Aunt Izzy who was stirring something in a big pot and shouted: "Back in less than an hour. I'll keep a low profile."

That meant skirting the public areas: the Res general store, the thrift shop, the small Catholic Church, a sleazy pawnshop, a combination gas and grocery store that advertised fishing and hunting licenses, and a shabby little café, The Res Resort.

Serendipitously, as I shot off toward the lake, I came upon a private area. Bright as a stoplight, Sue Ann's red Mercedes jutted out from the side of a dirt road that led into a thick grove of firs and pines. I couldn't see Sue Ann, but I did see a large white Stetson in what might appear to be a compromising position, considering the open passenger's door and the ostrich boots hanging out.

I cut to the left and headed toward the lake on what appeared to be a deer trail. Feinting and dodging like a reluctant boxer, I leapt over scraggly brush, a large downed Douglas fir, and planted my shoe into a pile of fresh scat—from a very sick bear or wolf. Ungulate hair and bone fragments glued themselves to the sole of my shoe.

I had been so preoccupied with what nasty business Sue Ann and Ebon Riley might be transacting in her father's car that I had forgotten to watch the path. Grabbing a large fir branch, I held it down with one foot as I dragged the yucky shoe back and forth across the prickly needles, caterwauling like an injured beast.

That's when I saw the blood, pooled by the side of the downed tree, and then splotched as bright as Christmas ornaments across a mat of fallen fir branches. The two pale blue eyes watching me from behind the log were neither terrified nor angry. They were exactly like Mother's eyes, too full of disbelief to register anything.

The old Victor coil spring animal trap had slashed into the front paw of what might be a husky or a coyote or a wolf and refused to release its prey. The creature huddled against the log—its welter of gray-tipped white fur shielding what must be a set of formidable teeth.

When I moved closer, a pink nose at the end of a long muzzle poked up, and two ears went on alert. A soft whine, the kind of noise Lorena makes in her sleep, vibrated in the silent forest, as though the wolf or dog was winding down from a long and painful ordeal.

It was. The spring-loaded trap sat squarely in front of me, its four-inch jaws clamped to a bloody white paw, its chain and a piece of rebar lying off to the side. Two small saucer-like tabs perched at each end of the jaws.

If I stood on each tab, the mouth of the trap should open. So might the mouth of the trapped animal. I looked down at my mesh running shoes. They were designed to breathe and would be no protection at all against sharp fangs.

I moved nearer. Those suffering blue eyes held more fear than malice. Inching closer to the trap and positioning my shoes so that I could step quickly on the release devices and leap back, I felt the hairs on my neck stand at attention. Something rough and wet slathered my hand.

It struggled to stand on three legs, increasing the bite of the cruel jaws of the trap. "Sit." I gave it the only command that made any sense. Oddly enough, it obeyed. It must be a dog, a well-trained dog, too small for a husky or a malamute, probably half-grown, around thirty pounds.

I knew next to nothing about dogs. We never could have a dog or a cat because of Lorena's asthma, although the kitten that Maylene gave Lorena didn't seem to cause her any breathing problems—until Marybeth tore into her with a switch and sent her stress up and her asthma into overdrive.

My friends in our old Portland neighborhood—when we lived as a nuclear family in a real house—had lots of needy, slobbery, smelly dogs. I preferred the arrogance of cats until this injured creature fixed his eyes on me as though I might be a reincarnation of the Good Samaritan.

I needed to talk myself and the dog through what might be another disaster. The trap looked old, rusty. It might not release when I stepped on it. It might bite harder into the paw. Then, the dog would bite me. I had no option.

The sun was setting. The Earnshaws would be worried about me, but I couldn't leave this dog in the forest. Injured and helpless, he would attract larger, hungry beasts.

"OK. This may hurt. You have to trust me to open this trap quickly. Don't move. Don't tear off my hand." I capped one hand firmly onto the nape of the dog's neck.

Easing the tips of both tennis shoes forward, I reared back on my heels and slammed the balls of both feet onto the left and right springs of the jaws. A sharp yelp pierced the silence—either from the dog or me; the mangled paw was free, and my hand was getting a tongue bath. I knew about emergency response, but the physiology of a dog's paw wasn't in my *Red Cross First Aid* book. The dog lay back down and waited to see what was next in store.

Jimi Hendrix. My new/used hoodie would serve as a wrap; I heaved up the dog, hoping it wouldn't go for my throat. It whined softly, closed its eyes, and nestled a pink nose into the pit of my arm.

Just at the edge of a clearing where the road forked toward the reservation stores, I headed toward a small, prefabricated house with a bright red door. A gaunt, middle-aged man bent over newly furrowed rows in a large garden at the side of the house and was dropping in onion sets.

Carrying thirty pounds of dead weight through an unfamiliar forest had exhausted me. I dropped down at the edge of his yard and shouted: "Can you help me?"

He dusted his hands off on his jeans, picked up his hoe, and came toward me with an unfriendly expression. When he saw the dog wrapped in Jimi Hendrix, he grinned warily. "Jimi sang 'Bleeding Heart,' not bleeding foot. That hoodie belonged to my son. Looks like you found a good use for it."

He squatted down beside me. "Let's take a look at that paw. Spring coil trap?"

I nodded, unwrapping the dog carefully, trying not to touch the bloody paw.

"Nasty things, those old metal traps. I don't think anyone uses them anymore. But, once they've been set, they're primed until some creature happens upon them. This little pup was lucky you found him. You keep rubbing the back of his neck to settle him; I need to see how deep this is."

The dog yelped sharply but didn't bare its teeth or try to move. "Hold on to him. I've got something inside that will help."

Within a few minutes, he came out with a bottle of distilled water, a tube of ointment, and a wad of gauze. "It's a deep cut, but I don't think he has broken bones." He dripped water onto the paw. "We'll put this ointment on it and cover it so it stays clean. There's a vet in town, but this wolfdog will probably get better on its own."

"Wolfdog?" I asked.

"Yeah. I'd say it's half husky or maybe malamute, but certainly half wolf. Look at its muzzle. Look at those feet. Very big for a half-grown pup. Ed Tomeh." He stuck out his hand.

"Jenny Ha . . ." *Whoops. I almost missed my cue.* "Jenny Earnshaw, Isabella Earnshaw's niece. Just visiting. I was on my run when I came across him. I don't know anything about dogs or how to take care of them. I don't think the Earnshaws have a dog."

"Sure they do. A half-wolf named Raven. Goes with Bill Earnshaw into the field. Not a good watchdog but a good companion."

Something about Ed Tomeh looked faintly familiar. Then, I recognized him. He wasn't sleeping on a grate or drinking out of a paper bag, but he resembled my Mr. Tomeh, the man who sometimes did odd jobs at the apartment where we lived in Portland, the man we often took dinner to on a paper plate, the man Mr. Darken kicked for blocking his way.

"Why don't you pick him up? I have a little pen around back where my old dog stayed. Died last year. Mixed breed. Best kind of pet. Not replaceable."

I rather liked the staccato beat of Mr. Tomeh's one-sided conversation and his take-charge manner. He swung a gate open, pulled a thick pad out of a small wooden doghouse, shook it, and motioned me over.

"This pup may belong to someone. You probably need to post something on the board in the general store. I can keep him until he's better. We need to watch that paw for infection. What do you call this lost fellow?"

*Nothing until Mr. Tomeh reminded me that an orphan deserves a name.*

"Pip," popped out of my mouth of its own volition.

"A wolfdog with great expectations," he grinned over at me.

I tried not to register surprise, but one eyebrow must have crept upward.

"Dr. Earnshaw. English Lit. She offers extension courses at the Tribal Center. For credit, or we can audit for no charge."

"Doctor? She never said that . . ." My foot was invading my mouth again. As a niece, I should know that my aunt held a doctorate. I didn't even know her husband's first name or that the family had a dog until Mr. Tomeh told me.

"Yeah. Both she and Bill. Doctorates but don't put on airs. Stanford. That's where they met. She grew up on the reservation, same class as my boy. Met Bill at Stanford. Now he speaks *'snchitsu'umshtsn'* better than many of us."

At first, I thought that Mr. Tomeh had just gargled. Then, I realized he was speaking another language. He turned on a hose bib, washed out a bowl, filled it with water and set it down by Pip.

"My own well water. Sweetest water on the Res. Have some." He handed me the hose. I managed to soak the Red Hot Chili Peppers; for good measure, I aimed a stream of water at my still-disgusting shoe. The late rays of the sun pierced the gaps between the Douglas firs lining his property, casting dark shadows along the road next to the house.

"I need to be on my way, Mr. Tomeh. Aunt Izzy will worry. I should have been home an hour ago. I'll come by to check on Pip tomorrow if that's OK?"

# CHAPTER 8

L ike little Pip coming home to his stern sister, Mrs. Joe, with her cane called the "Tickler," I fully expected to either be whacked or forced to drink Mrs. Joe's foul-tasting "tar-water" when I reached the Earnshaw front door.

The expression on Aunt Izzy's face rivaled either imagined punishment. "Ed Tomeh had the courtesy to let me know that you were on your way. I was just about to call the Tribal Police. Two rules, Jenny: you *always* come home at the time promised; or, if something delays you, you call home with a message. Understood?"

I nodded meekly. The last year in Portland with Mother working double shifts had left me to my own devices. I had to collect Lorena from school and keep her with me, but we were free to roam. Mother rarely got back to the apartment before ten o'clock. I had lost the habit of reporting my whereabouts.

Too ashamed to speak, I turned my head so that Aunt Izzy couldn't see my red face. Abusing her hospitality like this, giving her cause to worry made me hide my face in my hands.

"It's not the end of the world, Jenny. I've called the Tribal Police to find Heathcliff twice and Hareton once. Cathy, thank heavens, is not a roamer." She patted my shoulder. "It's just that you are at risk. Those CPRC people frighten me. Zealots are responsible for most of this world's woes."

The word "woes" struck a chord; tears actually splashed down my face. "I feel such a sense of rue, regret, contrition, repentance . . ."

Aunt Izzy interrupted by handing me a wad of tissue. "I only wish Heathcliff had your command of language, Jenny. He apologizes by saying 'Oh, Ma' and giving me a big hug so that I somehow feel complicit in whatever he's done."

"Whatever he's done wasn't worth the damn trip." A bootless Heathcliff had crept up behind us. "You look like the local waterworks, Jenny. Been up to no good?"

"I was ready to call the Tribal Police about you, too, Heathcliff. It doesn't take that long to drive to the Compound and back. Jenny's been out rescuing a dog. What have you rescued?"

Without waiting for an answer, Aunt Izzy put two bowls on the kitchen table. "Both of you sit. Mutton stew. My grandmother's recipe."

"Sheep eyeballs and hemlock, Jenny," Heath whispered in my ear, just a little too close for comfort. He frowned as his mother ladled thick, rich soup into the bowls. "You were right. They wouldn't let me in the gate. No one would check to see if Josh or his mother could talk with me."

He gulped soup greedily as I explained about finding the wolfdog and worrying his mother by being so late.

"She's a fiend about punctuality. Stew's better than usual, Ma. You got a good scald on this one." He shoved his chair back. "Nice appetizer. What's for dinner?"

She refilled his bowl. "More of the same. I'm on Spring Break. I'm re-reading Trollope. His satire is so subtle. You would do well to study him, Heathcliff. What took you so long?"

"They stopped me at the gate to get one of the elders, even though I told them I was on official reservation business—any lie in the storm, right Jenny?"

I glared at Heath, trying to think of recent cock and bull stories I might have told—only a lie of omission to Mr. Tomeh about the other Mr. Tomeh in Portland.

"Old Bonner showed up with a face like a thundercloud and told me that only church members were allowed inside, and I should never come back. That's when Gomer Darken spotted me and came trotting over to the gate. He was all diplomacy and tact. Asked about you and pa, Ma. Never did ask about our visitor though. Said he might pay a visit to the Res one of these days."

Heath wiped his mouth on a flowery napkin, folded it into a perfect equilateral triangle, and added: "The man has beans for brains. Does he think we don't talk to each other? That we didn't know he and those elders came to see Ebon at the Tribal Office?"

Heath's account of the idiot elders wasn't getting us anywhere. I was longing for information about Mother and Lorena and, maybe, Josh. I decided to show off with a tasty bit so Heath could pick up a point or two about spying on people. "I saw Ebon Riley this evening. In the woods. With that princess."

The mouths of Aunt Izzy and Heath fell in unison. Bingo. I had their complete attention and the power to move hills; mountains would have to wait.

"You must be mistaken, Jenny." Aunt Izzy's dour expression made me wish that I had been.

"Not in the least surprised, Jenny." Heath's sly glance told me that he knew more than he should about the beaded octopus with her flawless complexion and what I imagined to be a perfect body under all those quivering fringes.

"Common gossip." Aunt Izzy declared in a voice that didn't sound convinced.

"Started before Ebon's wife took the kid and left. Been making the circles ever since. Sue Ann isn't the little girl who used to eat cookies in our kitchen, Ma. Her tastes have changed." Heath wandered over to the cookie jar and ate three oatmeal cookies before offering me a single one.

His mother stomped out of the room.

"She'll get over it in minute, Jenny. Mother likes to think of me doing the Horsetail Dance in beaded leggings with fake Eagle feathers hanging down my back— and Sue Ann in fringes. Grade school entertainment." Heath pushed the cookie jar toward me. "Fresh oatmeal raisin. I'm surprised Hareton hasn't eaten all of them."

He leaned over toward me as though we were in collusion. "I'll tell you what I did see at the Compound. I drove on a side road to a place that has a stile across the fence leading off Compound land. It's fairly well hidden, but Josh showed it to me once. The women cross over to get to blackberry vines."

He eyed the remaining cookies and snapped the lid down. "Hareton's share. I skirted along a thick border of chokecherry and sumac toward the backside of some of the houses with that big field behind. I could see the Barnes's house clearly. Josh's pickup was in the drive on blocks with no tires in sight. We both learned how to drive in that old pickup. Josh's father taught us."

Heath's digressions were irritating me. "What about Josh? His mother? Any sign of them?"

"Nope. An officious-looking woman with a face like a spitting llama came out the back door a couple of times shaking rugs as though she might be taking out her frustration on them."

*Marybeth. What in the world would she be doing at Mrs. Barnes's house? Helping out? Spying? That was more likely.*

"The men were coming in from the fields, so I had to get out of there. I left Josh a message though."

"A message?"

"I don't know if he'll think about it, but when we were kids, we made ourselves a tree house not too far from the stile. You have to fight blackberry brambles to get to it. We must have been tougher as kids." Heath held the backs of two scratched hands toward me.

"I put a note under a rock up high on one of the old two by fours. Told him you were safe, fully recovered, and we are taking care of you. I also told him that you were very worried about your sister and mother."

"Josh would have to be clairvoyant to know you'd left him a note in a place you haven't visited since you were kids." My disappointment rang out louder than I intended.

At that moment Aunt Izzy appeared in the doorway; Heath stood up, unbuckled a wide Western belt, and popped open the top button on his jeans.

As I was reluctantly averting my eyes but dying to see the rest of this strip tease in his mother's kitchen, Aunt Izzy blurted out: "The tail of your shirt is gone! Blackberry bushes couldn't have done that."

"Nope. I tied a flag onto the stile. This is Josh's shirt. We traded last year. He liked that dumb flowered cowboy shirt you bought me. He used to work horses in that pasture by the stile. I thought he might see the cloth. I couldn't come up with a better idea."

He turned toward his mother and added gravely: "I saw a couple of men with Uzi carbines near the Compound gate. That week before his father died, Josh told me something in confidence. Sounds as though the secret might be out now. He said that the some of the men were stockpiling weapons, not shotguns or rifles, but AK 47s and Uzis."

Heath turned a thoughtful face toward both of us. "When I was at our old tree house, I suddenly remembered something that Josh told me when we were kids. He said that the original settlers in the 1840s, the ones who'd had some skirmishes with our tribe, had found a secret tunnel that led out of the area in case of a raid. They continued to keep it stocked with provisions—that mentality about preparing for the Apocalypse.

"Here's the weird part. The location was a secret. They didn't want people taking stuff out of there. So, the senior elder knew the location; he would tell only his oldest son. That went on for a few generations. During World War I, the head elder's son didn't come back from France. His father had a heart attack when he got the telegram. No one else knew the location of the tunnel. Could be fiction. Might not even exist. An old wives' tale."

"I don't want you poking around in the Compound, Heath. It's not safe. We need to come up with a plan to get Jenny's mother and sister—and Josh and his mother if they want to leave. When your father gets back from New Mexico in a couple of weeks, we will figure out something."

Aunt Izzy pulled a stool next to me and settled down for what might be the long haul. "In the meantime, Jenny, we need to do something about school for you. Just from talking to you, I know you excel in math and English, but you need credits on a high school transcript and early placement options. I've decided the best option for now is at the Tribal Education Center here on the Reservation. I've cleared it with the director." Her uneasy smile didn't get an answering one from me.

"When I said you were eighteen to keep people from questioning why an underage niece had come to visit, I didn't think about school. The director says you can take math, writing, and reading tests and do independent study for credit. You can sit in on GED classes if you like. She suggested that if any one is curious, you're simply making up some missed credits. She'll keep your transcript under your real name in her office. The teachers will think you are an Earnshaw."

The bloom was off the rose. Not that I didn't like school. I did. Just not now. And not here. I had to work out my own plan to get Mother and Lorena. Two weeks was too long to wait before taking action.

As to waiting for Aunt Izzy's husband to help with decisions, I wasn't sure that a forensic archeologist who studies traces of ancient wounds and long-ago diseases in old bones was the warrior I needed on my side. But, I was too polite to say so. So I said what I thought was expected of me. "School sounds like a great idea!"

"Why did that just remind me of Pip?" She laughed. "The character. Not your dog." She turned on her stool and looked unflinchingly into my eyes. "Pip was thinking that he had not been honest with his friend Joe and said that 'all of the swindlers on Earth are nothing to the self-swindlers.' You can't fool me, Jenny. You are not excited about school."

Heath butted in to save me from another lie. "If it isn't annoying enough to be named after Brontë characters, our failings are constantly being compared to oddball people in Dickens. Mom thinks that life is a Victorian novel. Get used to it, Jenny."

In spite of his snide comments when I told him and Aunt Izzy about seeing Sue Ann with Ebon Riley in the woods, Heath appeared edgy, ill at ease. Teasing his mother restored his good humor, but he couldn't quit drumming his fingers.

"I admit that I have Victorian sensibility. I don't mean in the common sense of prudishness. And you can quit rolling your eyes, Heathcliff!" She thumped his arm.

"Victorian sensibility is reformist and speculative. They had an enduring belief that literature can help us find meaning. When I relate literature to my everyday life, I'm a better teacher. I can help my students understand that what I teach is pertinent, relative to their own lives." She turned a defiant face toward Heathcliff and me.

It seemed the perfect moment to mend my lazy ways. I scooped up dirty bowls and headed toward the sink. "You cooked; I clean, Aunt Izzy. Go read Trollope. I intend to start *The Way We Live Now* tomorrow." I knew nothing about Trollope novels, but that one was on my bedside table, and the title struck me as fortuitous.

# CHAPTER 9

The clanging sound outside my window barged in on a dream. Zion Chapel bell resounded woefully as black-clad elders traipsed past a giant double-hinged coffin. Mother, with blue eyeliner rimming wide-open eyes, smiled up at me out of one side. In the other coffin, a small girl was facedown, her hair a tight mass of Shirley Temple curls.

A disembodied voice that sounded like mine repeated over and over: *hide your face so it won't be real.*

"Are you ever going to wake up, Jenny? Mama says we can go with Heath unless you want to sleep in. You don't do you?" The cocoa-colored sheaf of Cathy Earnshaw's ponytail dangled inches above my face as I groggily prized my eyes open.

"I spe-cif-i-cally," she stressed each syllable with perfect little lips covering teeth that seemed to be outgrowing her mouth, "deserted my best friend Stella so that I could spend quality time with you before school starts next week."

At nine, she was taller than my little sister, but Cathy bounced on my bed with the same disregard that Lorena had for anyone trying to sleep. "If you get up this instant, Jenny, I'll bring you a cup of coffee. Mama said I could. *If* you get up."

She was a bossy little thing and made me terribly lonesome for Lorena. I reached up and pulled her down beside me so that she would stop jiggling the mattress. Getting up too early inclines me toward motion sickness.

"I'm very pleased that you want to spend time with me, Cathy. If you can lie absolutely still without moving a muscle for two minutes, I'll take you to see something very interesting." I was thinking about Pip. I had promised Mr. Tomeh that I'd come by to see how he was getting along.

"The wolfdog you found? Mama already took a sack of Raven's dog food over to Mr. Tomeh this morning. She wouldn't let me go with her." The petulant expression on Cathy's face could rival Lorena at her sulky best. "I'd rather go with you, anyhow. After we catch a salmon."

Health yelled, but at least he didn't push his way into my bedroom. "Rise and shine, Jenny. They say salmon are running down by Wolf Lodge Creek. If Mother doesn't have grilled salmon once a week, she gets really testy."

I could hear Aunt Izzy lecturing Heath through the bedroom door. By the time Cathy pushed carefully through the door and dribbled coffee across the floor, I had brushed my mop of hair into some semblance of order and squeezed into the too-tight jeans. A pile of plain t-shirts, probably Hareton's and an oversized sweatshirt had replaced my bloodstained clothes from the wolfdog encounter.

"You don't have to go with Heath and Cathy unless you want to, Jenny. You seemed restless last night. Bad dreams?" Aunt Izzy handed me a warm tortilla filled with scrambled eggs, cheese, and sausage. "My version of Mc's breakfast burrito. My kids like to eat on the go."

She added steaming coffee to my cup. "When Heath was at the stables this morning, one of the guys said he caught some big salmon yesterday up by Wolf Lodge, close in since it's still cold. Grilled salmon from our lake is the best you'll ever eat. I invited Mr. Tomeh for dinner tonight when I took him a spare sack of dog food for your pup."

"I feel like a sluggard, Aunt Izzy. Everyone is up. You took food to Pip. You're feeding me, and all I can manage to do is disturb you with my bad dreams. I need to do something to earn my keep. Two of the reading lamps in the front room have gnarly plugs. I'll fix those for you today."

"Just *keep* this child of mine out of trouble at the lake." She frowned down at Cathy's very short shorts. "Sometimes I think Stella is a bad influence. Get on some long pants."

Aunt Izzy followed us outside and wiggled the safety chain on the boat that was hooked to an open jeep covered with more rust than paint. Cathy was in the back seat with some dirty orange life jackets on her lap and one very bare leg tucked under her.

"All of you wear your life jackets. That means you too, Heath. This time of year, hypothermia can do more damage than the plague. Stay close to the shore. No joy riding in that sorry little tub you call a boat. It will be breezy on the water." She handed me the big sweatshirt.

As we headed out on the main road, Heath waved toward a nearby mountain range. "Eagles nest over by that end of the lake in winter. We'll probably see them fishing. It's awesome when they snare a big one."

In between the grinding of gears, the reverberation of a boat that seemed ill fitted to its hitch, and Cathy's rendition of Taylor Swift's "I Knew You Were Trouble," I could do no more than try to appreciate the scenery. It was breathtaking even without eagles: an achingly blue sky and mountains framing a picture-perfect lake in the distance like a Chamber of Commerce ad.

The screeching, off-key voice pelting us from the back seat with "you've got me alone . . . you found me . . . you found me" reminded me that Lorena and Cathy shared a love of Taylor. Perhaps I needed to talk with Aunt Izzy about auditing some of her songs. Nine-year-olds and seven-year-olds should not be singing about bad boys that "flew them to places" they'd never been.

Those "places" ought to be the domain of an older sister, a new cousin. I checked out the profile of Heath. Artful. Determined. Like Alexander the Great at the top of his game—before he got feverish at Nebuchadnezzar.

Heath whipped the wheel of the old jeep with the expertise of an Indy driver and backed down a narrow concrete ramp leading into the lake. I had visions of being entombed in a rusty jeep at the bottom of the lake with the boat—bottoms up like a scavenging duck, marking our watery grave.

"Hold it while I park the jeep." Heath tossed me a rope; I struggled to keep my running shoes out of the lake, as the boat bobbed like a fishing lure. Cathy tossed in three life jackets, climbed up and sat in the bow like the wife of Poseidon, queen of all she surveyed.

If getting out of bed too fast in the mornings could make me queasy, a ride in a small boat over tsunami waves sent my breakfast burrito over the side as fish food.

"You're not much of a sailor," Heath laughed. "We'll stop here in this little nook of the bay to give you a breather. The water is only about thirty or forty feet here. If we spring a leak, we can practically walk to shore."

I clutched the life vest tighter and retied the strings. One tiny issue that I had neglected to mention: I can't swim. Never learned. Keep my bath water no deeper than a foot. My nerves were making me think in the same staccato rhythm as Mr. Tomeh's speech just as an arctic wind from Canada blasted us.

Showing off, Heath took off his jacket and pushed up his sleeves. *Nice biceps.*

"Salmon don't go out to the center of the lake where it's deeper at this time of year. Too cold. We'll be rocking a bit with the waves. You should be fine, Jenny."

I was until Heath drug half-frozen baitfish out of the cooler and started ramming his knife behind the small gelatinous gills.

"Has to be plug-cut to spin." He proudly held up something attached to a wicked hook, as though he might have just carved the Pieta out of prime marble.

I gagged and tried to avoid breathing until he latched the cooler lid. Cathy's bare legs had gone from a nice peachy tan to a bluish gray shade. She moved from the bow next to me and snuggled close. She might pay attention to her mother next time she heads to the North Pole in shorts.

"Let me make a suggestion," Heath eyed us both sympathetically. "Cathy is freezing. You're green around the gills. I'll just pull into the cove over by that old boat dock. You two get out, warm up in the sun, and I'll try to catch a fish for Mother. I don't dare come back empty handed. She's invited Mr. Tomeh for salmon. That means I show up with dinner or else."

The ramshackle dock angled at half-mast might appeal to a photographer, but it was a royal pain to hoist ourselves up from an unstable boat that might tip us into a thirty-foot depth at any moment.

A rusty tin can, silted in, and the frame of a folding chair a foot below the side of the boat comforted me. Solid land was no more than knee-deep below me.

Heath cranked the small engine, pushed off from the dock, and sped away with the front end of the boat climbing straight up off the tempestuous lake. I dared not watch such foolhardy behavior.

"I know a really good game, Jenny. Sister Margaret taught it to us. It takes more people to play it, but we could modify it for you, me, and Heath."

Drugged from the sun and secure on the warm, weathered planks of the old dock, I fought sleep as I struggled to listen to Cathy's reedy voice.

"It's called Hooks and Ladders. Some of the kids are the turbines in hydroelectric dams; some are pike minnows trying to catch salmon smolts; some are wildlife after the salmon; some are humans in boats fishing; and, best of all, some are the salmon. Sister Margaret lets us use the big slide as a salmon ladder; then, we can whiz down the slide to escape bears and fishermen."

Her thin voice peaked with enthusiasm. "Let's find something we can use for a ladder. We can put one end in the water here to make it more real."

Just like Lorena when her fantasy world got the better of her, Cathy was cranking herself up faster than a two-stroke engine. My nausea subsided, but my body wouldn't part company with the warm dock. I was in no mood for fun and games with a nine-year-old about the lost cause of salmon.

"Look! Look! He's caught one!"

In spite of his mother's warning, Heath had positioned the boat legions of feet from the shore, almost in the center of the lake where a depth of over 200 feet waited to claim the careless.

A shaft of silver at least a yard long spanned his upheld hands as a shout went up. "Dinner! I catch; you clean." He revved up the motor and cut a beautiful isosceles triangle wake onto the face of the now-calm lake before heading into shore.

Fish guts? I don't think so. Nice orange fillets from the meat market. I could handle those. Except for the sound of the motor splicing a current behind the boat, the silence was eerie. Cathy had disappeared.

I spotted her several yards from the old dock, struggling to pull something out of a pile of debris that had washed up on the shore. "I found the perfect thing, Jenny! For our game. Heath can be the fisherman."

Some games are too obvious. Someone back at the Compound had confiscated my Nintendo when I was hauled off in a drug-induced coma to the Winners' house. Mario's evil mushroom world was a comfort compared to the machinations behind the Compound gates.

The smack of metal on wood grated on my nerves in a way I couldn't explain. "What are you doing, Cathy?" I peered over the side of the dock at a barelegged child who was intent on angling the back half of a stepladder into the water and leaning the top against the dock. Only two rusty spreaders linked the remaining rails.

"It's a perfect salmon ladder! We can start the game!" she shouted as muddy water swirled around her tennis shoes.

The voice was Cathy's but the image that flashed before me was of Lorena, so far away, so lost.

"Get away from that thing, Cathy! Now! The spreaders are rusty. It won't hold you!"

The impish face grinning up at me sparkled with mischief just before two bright, brown eyes widened in apprehension.

# CHAPTER 10

The rasp of rusty metal was soft as a whisper. Cathy's shriek could wake the dead. Moving with a jolt of adrenaline, I flung myself over the edge of the dock, pried metal fragments off Cathy, and lifted her out of the muddy water. She stood on one leg, clutched me in a death grip, looked down at her other leg, and wailed.

Blood from the gap in her thigh flowed down her muddy leg like a dripping faucet. I knew what should be done; I simply didn't have clean gauze to do it. If I could just sort out the compartments in my brain where I kept the *Red Cross First Aid* book, I'd know exactly what to do.

I swooped her up as though she weighed no more than Lorena's kitten and headed as fast as I could run toward the jeep, parked about fifty yards away. "You'll be fine, Cathy. I'll take care of you."

In a voice that wanted to scream for Heath, I managed to keep it low and controlled. *Don't stress the injured. Get pressure on the wound.* With one hand, I yanked my sweatshirt up, trying to pry Cathy's arms from around my neck, so I could get it over my head.

"I'm going to put you in the back seat of the jeep; you need to lie flat with your leg up on the window ledge. I'll hold my shirt against the cut. It might hurt for just a minute, but I have to press very hard."

I turned my muddy sweatshirt inside out. An antiseptic field was out of the question considering the state of her grimy leg and my dirty shirt. "I'm going to shout very loud so that Heath can hear me. You don't need to be frightened, Cathy."

I was frightened enough for both of us. The sweatshirt was spongy beneath my palm. Blood oozed; it didn't spurt, so she hadn't severed an artery.

"Heath! Heath! Heath!" Like that of a mad bull moose, my blood-curdling bellow traveled across the lake and beyond. I tore my gaze away from Cathy, and there he was, pulling the boat halfway up the ramp and sprinting toward us.

"Great God in Heaven's name, what did you do, Cathy?" For once, there was not a trace of the sardonic expression Heath usually wore. The color drained from his face as he touched the blood-drenched sweatshirt I was holding against his sister's thigh.

"She needs a tourniquet! Here. My belt!" He whipped off his embossed western belt and waved it frantically.

"No! No tourniquet. She probably cut some veins but not an artery. You'll damage the tissue. We need to get her as fast as we can to the closest ER. I'm keeping pressure on it." I shoved his belt away as he tried again to loop it around Cathy's leg.

"Move the damn belt, Heath. I know what I'm doing. Don't put that around her leg!" I smacked his arm as hard as I could, causing him to stagger back with a shocked look.

Heath handled horses masterfully. He hauled in large salmon with aplomb. He did not function well with an injured sister. He rushed down to the boat and began pulling it up the ramp. I had the feeling that if I didn't intervene, he'd simply drag the boat all the way back home.

"Leave it, Heath! Get in the jeep and drive!" He responded well to orders, grinding gears, spinning around curves, driving down the middle of a main highway and honking at everyone whether they were in the way or not.

TWELVE STITCHES AND an hour later, Cathy was licking a lemon safety lollipop and explaining to her mother why Hooks and Ladders might not be her game of choice. "I wanted Heath and Jenny to play it with me, but they didn't pay any attention to the rules," she said peevishly.

"We'll wheel her out to the car now. This young lady will be fine as long as she stays away from rusty ladders." The ER nurse eased Cathy to a sitting position. "We gave her something for the pain and a tetanus booster. She'll probably sleep for several hours. You have her care instructions and a script for the pain meds, Dr. Earnshaw? She may not need it. Kids are very resilient."

Cathy didn't look the least bit resilient as her lids drooped. Every stitch the doctor made in that ragged cut had pierced my heart like one of those Renaissance paintings of Saint Sebastian impaled by arrows; I felt as weak with pain as he looked. I didn't guard her closely enough. Aunt Izzy should send me on my way. She had asked me to watch over her daughter; I couldn't manage the simplest request.

At that moment the ER doctor who had stitched up Cathy's leg stuck his head in the room. "Just checking on Cathy before she leaves. She's lucky that this young lady knew exactly what to do. She kept her leg up and applied pressure. You wouldn't believe the damage people do with misapplied tourniquets." He patted me on the back.

Heath ducked his head as though he'd like to be somewhere else, but he didn't say a word about our little disagreement.

Cathy grabbed my hand and pulled me next to her wheelchair. "I want Jenny to push me. She deserves a treat. She told me to leave that old ladder alone, but I didn't mind her. I will next time, Jenny. I promise." Her face drooped, then brightened as I edged the nurse aside and pushed the wheelchair down the hall and out the door.

"Heathcliff, why don't you take Hareton to get the boat. And the salmon. I hope you put it in the ice chest?" He nodded glumly. "Filet it down by the dock. I don't want fish guts in the house. Mr. Tomeh is coming for dinner, and Jenny's doing the grilling, right?" She squeezed my arm.

Aunt Izzy seemed to be putting up a good front for a woman who looked as though she might pass out when she first saw Cathy's leg. She maneuvered the car out of the Emergency parking lot and whipped it onto the highway leading back to the Reservation. At a red light, she turned to look at me in the back seat.

"I'd appreciate it if you'd give my boys a crash course in first aid. The nurse told me that you knew exactly what to do and why to do it. She said you could quote the *Red Cross First Aid* book from memory."

"I had to. My mother faints at the sight of blood. She goes ballistic over skinned knees. Lorena is clumsy. I had to know first aid," I added modestly.

"Heath told me that he would have fastened his big leather belt around her leg so tightly that the blood would stop flowing. That's all he could remember from his Cub Scout days. The doctor said that would have been a bad mistake." She smiled at me in the rearview mirror after she pulled through the intersection. "We're very lucky to have you in our family, Jenny. I hope that you know that."

All I knew was that for the first time in the past couple of hours, my stomach no longer clenched with pain, and my heart felt as though I had just had a very healthy transfusion. I would make myself useful to this family. Aunt Izzy was bound to like the way I grilled salmon if only she had a cedar plank.

# CHAPTER 11

Aunt Izzy left two cedar planks soaking in one side of the double sink. At my insistence, she had gone into the living room to placate Cathy, who snapped out orders faster than any child under the influence of codeine should be able to manage.

I poked around in the subzero refrigerators. The Earnshaw larder didn't have a year's worth of color-coded, dated food like Mr. Darken's kitchen; it was a mishmash of enough food for a small army with no single organizing principle. That was another thing I could do for Aunt Izzy, but not tonight. Tonight I was the chef.

"Just shout if you can't find things, Jenny. An organized kitchen isn't my forte. My office files are masterfully managed; it's a skill I haven't translated to hearth and home," she waved her hand as though to encompass messy cabinets and an overflowing countertop. "Garlic bread is in the freezer in the garage—right on top, I think. I do have a method of sorts."

If someone had taken a grocery cart of assorted frozen foods and turned it bottom side up into a small freezer, they'd have mastered Aunt Izzy's method.

In our tiny apartment in Portland, we needed no method. The freezer compartment in the thirty-year-old refrigerator housed a glacier of ice. We could store two frozen pizzas or ice trays. Like Europeans, out of necessity, Mother, Lorena and I favored warm beverages.

Being the sole cook for the first time in weeks gave me a different kind of independence that I'd missed. Mr. Darken's wives, Maylene and Marybeth, lorded it over everyone in the kitchen. Mother, Lorena and I were allotted the washing up detail, by hand, as though an automatic dishwasher might be an instrument of the devil.

Aunt Izzy was on the side of the angels with hundreds of kitchen tools—dozens of knives, all dull; every kind of grater known to man; shelves of spices, most of them out of date. I peeled two frozen loaves of garlic bread out of foil wrappers, scraped off the nasty spread, and smoothed freshly squeezed garlic and real butter on the loaves.

The vegetable drawer of the refrigerator bulged with greenery. We'd have a salad, boiled new potatoes that I would lightly sauté in olive oil with fresh parsley, and the pièce de résistance—salmon grilled on cedar planks.

Heath had made himself scarce after bringing home the boat and half a dozen salmon fillets. He walked sheepishly into the kitchen as I checked boiling potatoes and drained the lettuce. I could multitask in the kitchen—unlike Mother who was addicted to one-dish meals, macaroni and cheese being her specialty.

"I started the grill, Jenny. Least I could do, considering you're the hero of the hour and I'm the class dummy."

Heath was obviously still smarting from the tourniquet standoff. Or maybe I had smacked his arm harder than I intended. Stress can create a powerful adrenaline rush, an uncontrollable fight or flight response.

"I didn't mean to hit you so hard, Heath. I was over-reacting. I'm really sorry."

His snort was one of disbelief. "I'm an amateur boxer, Jenny. We have a gym here on the Res. I doubt that you could floor me." A wicked little grin spread across those perfect lips. "You could try. That might be fun." He flicked a strand of hair back off my face, letting his hand linger too long.

"If you're looking for entertainment, you could set the table, Heath. I'll fix a tray for Cathy. When Mr. Tomeh arrives, I'll start the salmon." I needed to be all business around Heath. He was just a bit too familiar. And a fainthearted girl like me might be at risk.

CATHY'S SOFT SNORES from the living room couch comforted everyone. As a patient, she proved to be difficult—demanding and whiny.

As the salmon paled to a perfect opaque on the grill, Aunt Izzy put on Beethoven's *Eroica* as poetic, sensual and mathematical background music. A spirited conversation was underway at the dinner table by the time the "Funeral March" began.

"For crying out loud, Ma, we don't need hearse music after a day like today." Heath seemed distracted before his outburst, just listening but not participating in the conversation. He shoved back his chair and went into the living room. Within minutes, Django Reinhart's "Lady Be Good" jazzed up the world.

"Hot club jazz," Mr. Tomeh announced. "Tull's favorite. Tull thought Django was the best jazz musician ever. I still have all of Tull's records. Don't listen to them."

I gasped. I just remembered something else about the Mr. Tomeh at our Portland apartment. For now, I needed to keep it to myself.

"We can put on something else, Ed. Or just talk." Izzy nodded at Heath and gestured toward the living room.

"No. I like the music. And the company." Mr. Tomeh beamed across the table at me. "And the cook." As a dinner guest, Mr. Tomeh was superb. He raved about the fish; he downed three small plates of salad; he said the potatoes were the best he'd ever eaten; and, he polished off half a loaf of store-bought bread, after subtly scraping off excess garlic slivers.

"You should check on Pip. He's a melancholy pup. Needs his owner. His paw looks fine."

Mr. Tomeh smiled across at me; then, his face dropped. "The music reminded me of Tull, my brother, Jenny. He took off exactly ten years ago today. We had words about . . . a bad habit. When my wife got the cancer, I couldn't locate him. He probably thinks she's still alive. In some ways, his not knowing gives me comfort."

The conversation had taken a turn toward intractable grief. I knew that road well. Every time I thought of my father, Mother, or Lorena, I only wanted to take steps backward, to reverse time, to circumvent what had happened to our lives.

If Einstein's paradox about the non-aging twin who travels in space and the aging twin who stays home had any truth to it, I could imagine being hurled backward not forward in the time/space construct and taking a different fork in the road. I'd counsel Mother about her spending habits. I'd chain myself to the wheel of my father's semi before I'd let him drive away.

I looked across the table at Mr. Tomeh. Except for a healthy, ruddy complexion and a freshly ironed shirt, he looked remarkably like the Mr. Tomeh that sat on the sidewalk back in Portland. He deserved to know. But not here. Not in front of everyone.

Some people might not like acknowledging black sheep in their families. Or drunks. Or missing uncles. Or nieces they didn't know they had.

"I'd best be on my way, Izzy. Still light outside. I thought the walk would do me good. Your hospitality has been fine. I don't get out much. I'm putting in a big garden this year. I'll bring you some produce one of these days." Mr. Tomeh headed toward the back door.

I grabbed the screen before it could swing shut. "Wait a minute, Mr. Tomeh. Do you mind if I walk with him, Aunt Izzy? I want to check on Pip. Can't be more than a mile. I'll be back before it gets dark. I'll clean up the kitchen then."

"Heathcliff and Hareton will clean up the kitchen. You walk with Mr. Tomeh. You can tell him about how you came to be my niece. He never talks out of school."

We'd taken a back route along the edge of a small field, neither of us saying a word until Mr. Tomeh grabbed my arm and hissed: "Ute ladies-tresses."

I whipped around, searching for something tribal with hair.

"There. Three of them. Wonderful. Very rare here." He pointed to some tall stalks with white flowers that I might have mistaken for gladiolas. I looked closer. These were so delicate and perfect, inching out of their stalks toward the light; they shamed flamboyant gladiolas.

He pulled a little notebook out of his pocket, scribbled in it and steered me back to a deer trail. "There's a lady with the Forest Service that keeps this kind of information. I let her know when I spot one of the endangered plants. You can't relocate them to save them. They decide where they want to be."

The note of sadness in Mr. Tomeh's voice suggested that he might be discussing the location of something other than wildflowers. I decided it was time to spill the beans. I *was* one of those people who liked to talk out of school.

"About your brother, Mr. Tomeh." I wasn't sure how much I should tell him. About the Thunderbird in the paper sack? His bed in winter on a grate? That we sometimes gave him part of our dinner on a paper plate? Or that he had once helped me fix a ceiling light socket in the apartment building?

Work on an electrical appliance was neutral territory. I could dress up his help a bit. He did steady the ladder and hand me tools. "I think I know where your brother is."

The expression on Mr. Tomeh's face was exactly the same as when he had spotted the rare Ute Ladies-Tresses. Hesitant. Quite disbelieving. Then, almost hopeful.

"We lived in an apartment in Portland. Well, that was after we lived in a nice house before . . ." I stopped. Mr. Tomeh didn't look as though he would appreciate a digression.

"We knew a man named Mr. Tomeh. He did odd jobs around the apartment building. So did I. Electrical work." I couldn't keep from crowing a bit about my little skill set. "The first time I saw you . . . when you helped me with Pip, I thought you resembled the man outside our apartment."

"What do you mean, outside?"

Foot in mouth disease again. That's how I always thought of our Mr. Tomeh sitting with his back against the building, clutching a paper bag. Lorena and I always got a lecture from Mother up three flights of stairs on the evils of alcohol after we passed him.

"I don't know where he lives. I don't think he had a place in our building. The apartment manager is tight-fisted. He reduced our monthly rent because I did all the minor electrical work in the building—mostly cook tops and sockets. Mr. Tomeh did odd jobs, mopped the lobby and swept the stairs, that kind of thing."

"Tull would never . . . would not . . ." His voice trailed into silence.

"He's probably not your brother. At dinner, when Heath put on Django Reinhart, and you talked about your brother, I suddenly remembered when I was working on one of those recessed lights down in the lobby of the apartment. I'd taken our old boom box with one of my father's CDs of Ella Fitzgerald."

I stopped and reached for Mr. Tomeh's hand. He looked so lost. "The stepladder was rickety. Mr. Tomeh came over to hold it and hand up my tools. He said he loved to listen to jazz. Ella was singing 'Every Time We Say Goodbye.' He had tears in his eyes. I remember that."

"Could have been Tull, I suppose. He always got emotional about jazz. Especially when he'd had too much to drink. That's when he went to a dark place. Sorry, Jenny. Don't mean to speak ill of Tull. I'm in somewhat of a state of shock. Let's check on Pip. Dogs help ground us." Mr. Tomeh picked up his pace so fast that he might make a name for himself in racing circles yet.

Pip sprang to the side of the fence. When I opened the gate, he pounced on me; his big feet pushed against my chest; as he struggled to climb up into my arms, his doggy odor almost overwhelmed me.

"He's your dog all right. Make no mistake about that. He lets me pet him and check his paw, but never acts happy to see me. He's bonded with you. Wolfdogs tend to be one-person dogs. Pip has chosen you."

I rubbed Pip's head distractedly. "I don't think Aunt Izzy would let me . . ."

"What? Let you keep him? Raven has a pen close to where Heath keeps that old boat of his. He could stay there until Bill gets back. Raven has the run of the house. Wolfdogs don't always get on together. We can figure out something." He scooped up a can of dried dog food, reached into his front pocket, pulled out a plastic bag, and thrust a wrinkled gray piece of salmon skin toward me.

"You give him the treat. Look at his eyes. He hasn't taken them off of you. I'll ask Izzy. We go back a long way. I don't mind asking. I owe you. Even if things don't work out, I'm still indebted. I need the address of your apartment in Portland. I haven't decided what to do. I want to think on it."

WHILE MR. TOMEH was thinking on what he needed to do about a brother who might have gone over to the dark side, I trotted back toward Aunt Izzy's house. It had the welcoming lines of a Craftsman with massive beams holding up a broad front porch that led into the generous living room. Bedroom wings spanned an upper story on both sides of the entry.

Aunt Izzy and her husband collected Native American art—baskets, pottery, beadwork pouches, and rows of ledger drawings tucked back in a corner away from the light. Shelves lined every wall. More valuable items rested behind glass sliding doors.

Unlike a museum guard, Aunt Izzy had encouraged me to examine things. "Handle them, Jenny. That's the only way you can feel the spirit of the artist. We keep the beadwork behind glass so that Raven won't be tempted by the old leather, think it's one of his rawhide bones."

Generous to a fault, Aunt Izzy had moved a Fritz Scholder painting that I had admired into my bedroom.

"He's not exactly a traditional Native American painter, but the critics like him. He admired the Expressionists. He painted like an angry child with a palette of primary colors. A very talented, angry child." I had a feeling that Aunt Izzy might be making an inference beyond a style of painting as she hung it on the wall by my bed.

I COVERED THE distance back to the Earnshaw house in minutes. As I stopped to admire the way the setting sun cast long, shimmering rays that flashed off a two-story bank of front windows, I saw a snake in the grass. A very large snake in very tall grass.

A black Chrysler with dark, opaque windows pushed its snout out from clumps of ornamental grass just beyond the Earnshaw property line. I could hear the soft hum of its engine.

My first impulse was to run into the forest back to Mr. Tomeh's where no Chrysler could follow. My second impulse was to pretend I hadn't seen it, to saunter up the steps, find a gun and blow out its tires before I drilled the driver.

Heath stepped out onto the porch and smiled. "That was quick, Jenny. Preparing for your next 10-K?"

"That or jail. If you have a gun, I'd like to borrow it." I pushed past him into the foyer.

"Whoa. Guns and anger don't mix. What's going on?"

"Mr. Darken. That's his car down there at the end of the road. He's pulled back behind that tall grass, but it's definitely his car."

"Stay!" Heath pushed me back and shouted as though he might be commanding a dog. Grated on my nerves worse than fear.

"I'll check it out," he said rather smugly I thought.

While he trotted down the steps, I could hear tires squealing on gravel and see taillights bouncing along a pocked road. Heath turned and held up helpless hands.

# CHAPTER 12

Helplessness didn't enter my mind when I went to bed early. I was stoked. In a tizzle as the rappers put it. They said it more pointedly than I could: "I'ma busta cap in yo azz." Mr. Darken had taken his ass off into the dark. Heathcliff couldn't catch him, and I had no gun to "busta cap."

My head throbbed as I thought about what gangsta rap rage does to the soul. It's like lighting a piece of paper and watching the edges bursting with orange and red flames before it blackens. Only the bitterness of gray ash settles into a dirty smudge.

Ash is the residue of the bitterness a victim feels. That's why Martin Luther King sang out "We Shall Overcome" as a rallying cry to replace anger. Yet, he had criticized the country's leadership as they waited "for a more convenient season" to take action. That "seasonal" comment must have galled him beyond imagining.

The season for me to act was now, but I knew I must do it in the spirit of Euclid—by determining a single, logical and coherent framework for action.

Relief flooded over me as my anger subsided. I was in a sanctuary provided by the Earnshaws. They would help me rescue Mother and Lorena. They had their own bone to pick with the CPRCers regarding the death of Mr. Barnes and the confinement of Josh and his mother.

Abigail's mother was surely taking care of Lorena. And Mother? The thought of her pandering to Gomer Darken sent my blood pressure soaring.

I picked up *The Way We Live Now* off the bedside table. Trollope put me to sleep after an introduction to Melmotte and his schemes—the undercurrent of Jewish lending practices triggered thoughts of Shakespeare's Shylock wanting his pound of flesh. For once, when I thought of Mr. Darken, I was on Shylock's side.


I WOKE TO the sound of Aunt Izzy tapping on my door. "I'm running a few errands this morning and thought you might like to drop by the Education Center. It's one of the oldest buildings on the reservation. You can meet the director, Mrs. Evans, who will be giving you some tests next week."

Meeting the person who was going to give me a battery of tests sparked my interest about as much as an interrupted electric current. I might like seeing the oldest building. I envisioned a magnificent antebellum with imposing Doric columns or perhaps a sturdy stone copy of an English college with great circular staircases, grooved from the steps of academics traipsing up to their garrets on the top floor.

THE PLAIN SQUARED-OFF building made of cement ✓ blocks with a tin roof dashed my expectations.

"Were you expecting an Oxford College, Jenny? You look disappointed. This old building was constructed in the early 1900s. Our tribe takes great pride in the fact that our first public building was a school—we were a poor tribe. We still are. When we got a settlement from the Indian Claims Commission, most of that went to the Casino. It makes money. Provides scholarships for our kids."

Aunt Izzy bustled me past a sleepy receptionist who glanced up under hooded lids, walked me down a waxed corridor past several empty rooms to an office at the end, and shoved open the door.

Seeing a girl hunched over filling out a form stopped her in her tracks. "Sue Ann? What are you doing here?"

Sue Ann looked a little worse for wear. In jeans and an old sweatshirt with her hair twisted into a tight bun to hide its disheveled condition, Sue Ann's aura of a proud Indian princess had gone the way of the buffalo.

"Uh . . . I . . . Mrs. Evans . . . uh . . ." Sue Ann was having a hard time finding a verb this morning.

I smiled genially at her. I never had trouble with verbs or nouns or even gerunds. Catching a princess off her pedestal can be pleasurable.

She did not smile back. "Mrs. Evans offered to help me fill out some college applications. I told Daddy I want to try for modeling school. Later . . ." She watched the word "later" drop to the floor like the ash from a concealed cigarette and refocused her attention on a stack of papers.

"We'll see you at the powwow tonight, won't we Sue Ann? I know it's just a community gathering, but your father told me he had bought you a new Jingle dress and you would perform for us."

Aunt Izzy seemed fixated on getting the princess to put on her duds and hop around in front of the crowd. I couldn't do the two-step without stumbling. So, naturally, I would resent Sue Ann tripping the light fantastic in front of cheering spectators.

I could hotfoot it through a 10K at a passable speed; I could strip and splice electric wire with the dexterity of a card shark—not exactly a spectator sport. I was a hotshot at math, but Hareton was my only appreciative audience.

"Sure, Mrs. Earnshaw. I'll perform the Jingle dance. Will Heath be drumming?"

"He'll be there for the food. You know Heathcliff."

The flush charging Sue Ann's cheeks made me wonder just how well she knew Heath. She ducked her head and shammed fascination with the format of a college app.

"Izzy? I thought I heard your voice out here. Lou Evans, Jenny. Izzy told me a bit about you. I hope we can help." The woman who thrust out a hand might have stepped out of the 1616 portrait of Pocahontas. Standing away from her neck, the stiff ruff of her white lace collar framed a face the color of unbleached linen. Like the famous painting in the Smithsonian's National Portrait Gallery, the luminous brown eyes were chary of what they might be revealing.

"Sue Ann, when you finish the forms, you can just leave them in my in-box on the desk. I'll check them and call you if we need to review them again." As though she had just encountered one of those worrisome fruit flies, a faintly exasperated expression settled around her mouth. Then she turned a bright smile toward me. "Izzy says you've done algebra, plane geometry and a bit of trig with analytical geometry in your Portland schools. We can do the PSAT here. You might want to go with Izzy to Spokane to take the ACT."

She led us into an office with giant posters of a 2010 powwow plastered on the walls. The male dancers looked like mating birds, strutting around with feathers going every which way. I thought that Heath would make a stunning dancer. He had been dismissive about his mother's interest in his dancing. Sue Ann's question about him drumming piqued my interest.

Food seemed to be the only interest of Aunt Izzy and Mrs. Evans who spent the next half hour discussing what they'd bring to the powwow tonight. I knew about big, flashy powwows. Portland held an annual event with all the trappings of a circus. The powwow they were discussing sounded like a family dinner.

"Like a potluck?" I asked, trying to suggest an interest I wasn't feeling. The idea of a potluck gave me bad vibes. It was at the CPRC potluck that I met Elder Winner and came up with my plan to electrify the Compound gates—my failed scheme.

"Somewhat like a potluck, Jenny. Women bring the kinds of food that are part of our history—possum grape dumplings, dried corn soup, things like that—and we have a big outdoor grill for salmon and buffalo burgers. Burgers are a modern concession to keep the children happy. It's more than a potluck. We dance. Not fancy dancing. Unless Sue Ann shows off her new dress. I suggested it because she looks depressed about something."

Aunt Izzy pushed back her chair abruptly. "I almost forgot. Ed Tomeh called early this morning and said he was off to Portland. He said you'd know why, Jenny."

The quizzical looks that Aunt Izzy and Mrs. Evans turned toward me didn't get any response. The whereabouts of Mr. Tomeh's long-lost brother Tull was our secret until he revealed it.

"Well. That's between you and Ed," Aunt Izzy said decisively. "He said we should look after Pip. That's the wolfdog Jenny found out in the forest, Lou. He was caught in one of those old spring traps. He can stay out back in Raven's pen, Jenny. We'll swing by and get him." She gave Mrs. Evans a brief hug and hurried me out to her car.

"Mr. Tomeh said I should put up a notice in case he has an owner." I said with reluctance. The thought of someone claiming Pip made me feel as depressed as Sue Ann looked.

"I told Mrs. Masset at the Thrift Shop. She's the town crier." Aunt Izzy grinned over at me. "Word of mouth but at an exponential rate. Twitter and Facebook take a backseat to Mrs. Masset."

"Like Fibonacci's sequence," I thought aloud.

"An Italian painter?" Aunt Izzy guessed.

"No. Fibonacci discovered a simple numerical pattern that is the foundation for the mathematical relationship behind phi—the golden ratio."

Faint worry lines creased her forehead. "You'll have to make it more elementary, Jenny. Heathcliff does OK in math. Like his father, Hareton loves math. Cathy, I fear, takes after me. I can manage fractions, decimals, multiplication and basic math concepts. That's about it." She pulled the car to the front of Mr. Tomeh's house. "You've been a godsend to Hareton. I frustrate him when I try to help him with math—and Heathcliff always seems too busy."

I stepped out of the car, picked up a pinecone and put it in her hand. "Fibonacci in nature, Aunt Izzy. He's everywhere—on the head of a sunflower, in the displacement of leaves around a stem. When you start with 0 and 1, each new number in the sequence is the sum of the two before it. I can help Cathy, too. My little sister got Mother's I-hate-math-gene."

Tears flushed my eyes. I could bite my tongue for every harsh word I'd ever said to Lorena or Mother. Math was elegant. It couldn't replace affection. The arms holding me tightly at that moment wrapped me in the faintest odor of gardenias and belonging.

# CHAPTER 13

M r. Tomeh's warning about wolfdogs being a single owner canine didn't hold water. Limping in unison with Cathy, Pip was all over her and Hareton with big, slobbery licks to their faces. He kept a respectful distance from Aunt Izzy. Heath was nowhere to be seen.

"Sue Ann came by in her dad's Merc. Said they needed Heath down by the Tribal Center to help set up the grill and tables outside. He didn't look too excited at the prospect."

Hareton lowered his voice and whispered to me. "Sue Ann acted weird. She's usually mushy around me. She didn't even notice me standing by Heath. Weird."

"Lunch!" Aunt Izzy's voice rang out louder than Marybeth's dinner bell. Aunt Izzy had advised me that after lunch, she would be teaching me the culinary arts of Native American cooking—fry bread, possum grape dumplings and hominy soup.

It sounded like a toxic combination, but in the days before refrigeration, factory farming, and the great buffalo slaughter, they probably learned to make do—just as Mother, Lorena and I did with out-of-date frozen pizza. Toss on shop-worn, lightly sautéed broccoli (brown around the edges); trim away the onion's mushy outer layers and slice thin circles for the top. Bake. The only cost for the meal is electricity that is part of the apartment rent.

I mastered the art of fry bread quickly, dusted my batch with cinnamon and sugar, and offered the lot up to Hareton and Cathy. The grape dumplings were trickier because the possum grapes were frozen—"too wet" said Aunt Izzy. I passed on the hominy soup with rounds of baked mutton bones floating on top like something the butcher had discarded.

"It's the other kind of Indian soup—full of cumin and turmeric. We never had those spices in the past. Bill's mother taught me this recipe. Her grandmother learned it from her cook in India. I pretend it's authentic, because I love it so."

She pointed toward my bedroom. "Lou Evans dropped by a few things that her daughter outgrew. Thought you might use them."

The casual tone of her voice saying "dropped by" downplayed the fact that my wardrobe consisted of a few things Heath had bought at the Thrift Shop and Hareton's old shirts; I was at the mercy of hand-me-downs. I looked at my too-tight jeans streaked with grass stains from Pip's paws. Surely the clothes wouldn't look like the castoffs of Leah Winner's daughter—huge, droopy skirts and XXL blouses.

The stack of flirty skirts on my bed would have shocked Leah Winner—and her daughter—into a major

MI. The fluttery skater and rump-clamping skirts struck me mid-thigh. Two pairs of black tights would keep the evening breeze tolerable. I shook out a peasant blouse, two studded tank tops, and an over-sized see-through shirt. A cropped two-tone denim jacket could replace Jimi Hendrix at the powwow tonight.

CONDITIONED HAIR, DRIED with an actual blow dryer, made me feel presentable. Too much eye shadow and a frightfully short skirt might have been a bit over the edge had not Heath been watching with appraising eyes.

"You'd be runway material in that outfit, Jenny, if you had some Jimmy Choos or Manolo Blahniks instead of those old tennis shoes." Heath grabbed my hand and twirled me around in the foyer. "Can't say I don't like the black hose. Doesn't leave much to the imagination."

"If your imagination doesn't get itself under control, you will be having a conversation with your father when he gets home. A few weeks of digging in the desert lowlands of New Mexico might be just the . . ."

"Oh, Ma! For someone who is a closet watcher of *Sex in the City* reruns, you should appreciate the fact that I know the difference between Jimmy Choo and Converse tennis shoes."

"I'll find you some nice little ballet flats in Spokane next week, Jenny. Heath, I suppose your drum is in the jeep, so you can load the food in the back of my car. I'll take Jenny and Cathy. You take Hareton."

The powwow on the grounds around the Tribal Center didn't resemble the segregated potluck at Zion Chapel's Community Room. Big spotlights from the front of the Center lit up an expanse lined with picnic tables. A ten-foot grill covered with burgers, hot dog links and salmon sizzled over a bed of graying lumps of charcoal, the bright red-orange below the ashes at a perfect pitch.

Men, women, teenagers, and children milled about in a large clearing, shouting, smiling, and hugging late arrivals with obvious affection.

Except for Ebon Riley. Wearing a stiff tan shirt, razor-creased khakis, and those brownish speckled ostrich boots, he reminded me of a thorny devil, *Molock horridus*, as he slithered purposefully from group to group, working the crowd, ducking his head with false modesty.

The thorny devil lizard has an unusual physique, an extra false head; when he meets a predator, he simply offers his false head as a snack and goes on his way.

"Ebon's after the CEO position at the casino. Never gonna happen. Not while I'm on the Council," Izzy's father growled into my ear. "Too much palavering with those saints you left behind, Jenny." I hadn't seen Aunt Izzy's father since he invaded my bedroom and helped himself to my breakfast. His arm around my shoulders was a special comfort tonight.

Ebon Riley gave me the willies. He looked at me so purposefully, as though he knew exactly where I was meant to be—and it wasn't on the Reservation.

"Hareton's found us a table over there by the clearing. I see Izzy waving to us. We don't stand on ceremony around here. Let's get in line before all of Izzy's dumplings disappear." Aunt Izzy's father tucked my hand under his arm and headed at a fast clip toward the tables of food. "You can call me Gramps. That's what my grandchildren call me."

His profile with its slightly aquiline nose was a dead ringer for Iron Eyes Cody. I remembered reading somewhere that the famous Hollywood Indian actor was the child of Sicilian immigrants. No matter, his single tear helped keep America beautiful.

As we neared the table, a jingle-jangle creation sporting cascades of tin cones that must number a thousand popped into view. Underneath the shiny jingles, the leather was dyed a shade of indigo blue that no Native American could have found in the wild. The princess was hanging onto Heath's arm.

Ebon Riley stood just inside the open door of the building, his eyes fixed on Sue Ann, but careful not to let anyone notice.

"Pa, you and Jenny need to get through the line and then get your meat. We're running low on burgers. Good crowd tonight. Sue Ann is sitting with us. Her father is out of town. She says she's not hungry and feels a bit faint. I made Heathcliff walk her over to the food table to see if anything would tempt her."

Having Sue Ann as a dinner companion didn't tempt me at all. Salmon grilled to perfection did. I worked my way through four eight-ounce portions, two pounds of the best fish I'd ever eaten with one small possum grape dumpling and a spoon of boiled greens.

"You're not likely to founder, Jenny. Not overloading on carbs like Hareton is." Gramps pointed to a heap of mashed potatoes sharing Hareton's plate with chocolate cake.

"Founder?" I knew what the noun meant.

Hareton grinned at his grandfather. "Jenny knows a lot about math and electricity and even how to cook. She doesn't know squat about horses. She actually thought Mom's green mare would be the color of grass."

While Hareton and his grandfather were having a fine time discussing my ignorance of everything related to a horse but the Latin word *equus*, bells were going off in my head and my heart was thumping like distant thunder.

HEATH AND TWO other drummers sat in the center of the circle hammering away and singing something that sounded more like a Gregorian chant than any live music I'd ever heard. The pale moon cast eerie shadows through a fringe of Douglas fir.

From just to the left of the circle, the tintinnabulation from a jangling phantom stopped all conversation as Sue Ann took center stage. It was magical. I hated to admit it, but it simply was.

The ambient glow from the downcast spotlights stilled the night as the stars dropped out of the dark heavens and circumnavigated the dance arena, sparkling in rhythm with the drums.

From the drum circle came a voice that I knew to be Heath's although it might as well have come from a medieval monk chanting in a single tone, flowing, even and intensely sad.

Without so much as a pause or a bow, Sue Ann moved away from the circle and into the shadow of the trees.

"Time for us, Jenny." Aunt Izzy tossed a bright shawl around my shoulders as I protested. "No fancy footwork, just a sideways shuffle. Easy."

Within minutes, I was linked in a loop with women and girls, shoulder-to-shoulder, shawls gripped in mummy-style hands. We moved slowly in one direction, step, drag, step, drag until my hips began to protest. Then, I was free of pain.

Under that canopy of stars, with the steady pounding of the drums and the voices of the drummers flung up to heaven, I understood this dance. It belonged to women. The movement, the cycle, was elemental as the tides and as perfectly designed as though Euclid himself had drawn the circle.

The fancy dancers with their feathers and shuffles and stomps, bending and arching, whirling like dervishes, were a prologue to the real spirit of the dance. These women, barely lifting their feet from the dirt understood the meaning of being grounded in the history of their past.

Then the drums stopped. I headed toward the Tribal Council building for a bathroom break.

One of the two stalls was locked and occupied by a dead giveaway. A cyanide blue animal's hide covered with odd tin cones hung over the front of the stall. From inside, I could hear the strangled sounds of retching. Having an eidetic memory, my recent pitiful state in the woods flashed before me. Josh had rescued me. I could do no less for Sue Ann.

I pried my fingers between the stall and door to lift the latch. "Sue Ann? It's Jenny. Can I help you?"

Embracing a grotty toilet stool with both arms and wearing only underwear, Sue Ann turned her tear-streaked face to me. "I don't think anyone can help me. I think I'm past help. My heart hurts. I think it's broken."

In a pinch, I could set a broken leg with sticks and tape. My heart had been broken twice—when my father died and when I left Mother and Lorena behind with the CPRC bunch. The only remedy I knew was time and small kindnesses.

I grabbed a handful of paper towels, thrust them under a gush of icy water in the sink, and mopped up Sue Ann's face and hands. Ruffling through her duffle bag, I found jeans, a shirt and shoes.

"Let's get you dressed and out of here. I beat the crowd after the dance was over, but I can hear voices coming this way."

For a sickly person with a broken heart, Sue Ann moved with the speed of dark matter—her face neither absorbed nor emitted light. She had closed down. I might have been one of the queen's lackeys as she brushed me aside, stuffing dyed leather and knee-high beaded moc-casins into her duffle.

# CHAPTER 14

Heading back toward the dance circle, I noticed that Sue Ann had drawn Aunt Izzy away from the crowd. In the floodlight, they cast an odd reflection. Sue Ann curved toward Aunt Izzy like the arc of a parabola. Aunt Izzy was the axis of symmetry, straight as an arrow, unmoving, as though she had been shocked into stasis.

At the corner of the Tribal Council building, I passed another watcher. Ebon Riley. A cigarette hung between his lips, a tube of gray ashes, humped like a diseased caterpillar. I could smell the faint odor of sulfur.

By the time I reached the table where Cathy, Hareton, and Gramps were polishing off the last crumbs of my slice of chocolate cake, Aunt Izzy was coming toward us in a dead heat, her cell phone rammed hard against her ear.

"Load up! We're going home. Now!" I had never seen Aunt Izzy in such a state. Her mouth folded into a grim line. "Hareton. Go get your brother and tell him we are leaving. Both of you come straight home."

Aunt Izzy's father stood, stretched lazily, and muttered: "Whatever is troubling you, Izzy, needs to let the sun rise and set on it. It will keep for a few hours while you think about it."

Gramps stretched a long, straight arm toward his daughter and touched her briefly on the cheek. Like one of Euclid's definitions, the line was breathless in length.

"I suppose it will, Papa. Though I doubt it will keep for long." She turned away with a disconsolate slump of her shoulders and piled dishes noisily into her basket.

Aunt Izzy didn't say a word as she drove home. Cathy whined that her leg was hurting, but I knew she was upset by her mother's silence. The minute we got inside, I hustled Cathy upstairs with the promise of a gruesome fairy tale. Rapunzel in her tower. I was feeling isolated by the silence but didn't think Aunt Izzy was up for our nighttime decaf.

Within minutes, Cathy was asleep. I could hear the back door slam and Hareton thumping his feet along the stairs, irritated that he'd been sent to bed.

My bedroom was the guest room, downstairs and close to the living room. I crept back down from Cathy's room as quietly as possible and stood in the doorframe in case I needed to be invisible. I was a competent eavesdropper, always have been. What people don't want to share is usually the only thing worth hearing. Skeletons dangling in closets are fleshed out with interesting secrets from people who think no one is listening.

The pine floors and waist-high paneling transmitted sound perfectly. I might as well have been on the top row of the ancient Greek theater in Epidaurus for such acoustical perfection. A classic drama unfolded in the living room and Jason, AKA, Heathcliff, was pleading his case. "She told me, Ma. She didn't accuse me. How could she?"

Aunt Izzy's voice was low and pained. I could hear only a few of her words, like slivers of sound through a grate, as though she didn't really want to ask any questions. "When?" rang out clearly. "What month?" followed on its heels.

Those hours I spent in Elder Winner's attic reading *The Bible* and *The Book of Mormon* had created some kind of obsession with Biblical figures. In the Compound, I had been Jonah in the belly of the whale. Now I was Saul with the scales falling away from my eyes.

The jingle-jangle princess was about to produce a little prince and planned to name him Heathcliff. The non-fictional Heathcliff was having none of it. His protests were loud enough to raise the roof—if the slamming of the back door didn't bring the entire house down around our ears.

I sat in the dark of my room holding Trollope on my lap. Marie Melmotte paled as a distressed character when compared to Sue Ann. All those troublesome laces and whalebone corsets were more of a deterrent than fringed buckskins.

The door inched open and a sliver of light lit up the limp hand with the fingers pinched as though holding something invisible toward me.

The strangest image popped into my head. I remembered the myth of Thetis, the nymph who dipped her half-human son Achilles by the heel into the River Styx to make him immortal. The heel she held made him vulnerable to the poisoned arrow—the bolt Sue Ann had just sent his way.

"Jenny, are you awake? Can you bear some company?" Aunt Izzy crept into the room, sat beside me on the bed, and poured out her grief without telling me exactly what Sue Ann had told her. I knew. It wasn't a mortal heel that made Heath vulnerable; it was testosterone, a male affliction.

"This thing . . . the thing that Sue Ann said put me off balance. She and Heath are only eighteen, born two weeks apart. Lila, Sue Ann's mother, was my best friend; we celebrated their first five birthdays together. Lila died thirteen years ago—a brain aneurysm. She always had headaches. When she said she was having the worst headache of her life, no one paid much attention." Aunt Izzy crawled behind me and stretched out on the far side of the bed.

"Then, it was too late. Do you mind if I just stretch out here on your bed? My heart feels weak." She trailed her fingers across my stiffening back. "Don't worry. I'm strong as a horse. I like drama in novels—just not in my family."

She grabbed both pillows and propped them under her head, sniffling softly. "You probably don't have the faintest idea about what's going on? Raised voices, door slamming, Heathcliff roaring out of here in that old jeep of his."

"Actually, I do." It seemed unfriendly not to stretch out beside Aunt Izzy, although she took up considerably more space than Lorena. I propped my head up against the slatted wooden headboard and tried to think about how much of my eavesdropping to reveal.

"I found Sue Ann puking in the bathroom earlier tonight. I helped her into her clothes. I didn't think the flu or food poisoning would cause her to have a broken heart."

"Broken heart?"

"That's what she said."

"Because of my son?"

"No. She didn't say that. She seemed anxious, distraught." I didn't dare tell Aunt Izzy that sound traveled through her walls better than a wiretap would.

My thoughtless mention of Sue Ann's anxiety brought on a fresh batch of sobs. I struggled for words to comfort Aunt Izzy and remembered Heath's last shout before he slammed out of the house: "I'm not the one!"

I gave her the same advice I would give my mother if I had been falsely accused. "You must trust Heath. He wouldn't lie to you."

As usual, I can never take the advice of that old fool Polonius that brevity is the soul of wit. So like Shakespeare to put all the wisest words into a stupid man's mouth. I just had to let my inner detective speak: "A paternity test can clear him immediately."

The wail that went up would have shamed a Banshee. The unorganized clutter of words that shot out of Aunt Izzy's mouth didn't seem venomous, but rather like that dirty river foam that pours into the ocean and shifts around next to land. Shame, public exposure, Heath's reputation, and an interrupted life seemed to be the gist of her fears. "I am so stressed that I just can't think straight, Jenny!"

So I provided the only restorative I could think of for a woman with math anxiety. It would be sure to put her to sleep. "Aunt Izzy, when I feel stressed, Euclid sets me straight. We can begin with his definitions: the extremities of a line are points; an obtuse angle is an angle greater than a right angle; a boundary is that which is an extremity of anything."

I was just getting to my favorites—the triangles—when Aunt Izzy's soft snores stopped me. She had flopped over on her side, wrapped herself in my blanket and with any luck wouldn't let a powwow into her dreams.

# CHAPTER 15

The sounds bouncing along the hall might have been coming from a Copland symphony rather than the Earnshaws. Finding that Aunt Izzy had left my bed sometime in the night, I pulled on my clothes and approached the kitchen.

Cathy's reed-like voice was oboe thin; Hareton's climbed up and down the scale like an out-of-tune viola; Heathcliff provided a steady, reassuring bass. Over the top of it all, I could hear Aunt Izzy as pure and clear as a French horn: "You kids are driving me up the wall! I'm ready to send you all to New Mexico. Your father can deal with you!"

The over-sized dog in the foyer fixed a cockeyed stare at me with one blue and one brown eye. The ruff on his neck stood at attention. I froze in my tracks.

The tall, muscular man with ruddy, sun-burnt skin standing next to the dog might have passed for a Native American had it not been for his thatch of copper-colored hair and eyes pale as a summer sky. He glanced over at me and grinned before shouting: "He will! Bring on the brats!"

Cathy shrieked and flung herself around her father's legs. "Daddy! Daddy! I need to show you my scar and that's Jenny over there and she knew what to do and Heath could have really hurt me with that old belt of his but Jenny wouldn't and he couldn't and . . ."

Bill Earnshaw pried Cathy off his legs, hugged her, and set her down by the dog. "Raven's been missing you, Cathy." He grinned over at me again as he watched his daughter pile into that statue of a dog that looked more like the Egyptian god Anubis than a family pet. "Fickle little thing, isn't she?"

Just before Aunt Izzy and Hareton hurled down the hallway like a pair of guided missiles, he stuck out a calloused hand and grabbed both of mine in a single grip. "Couldn't wait to meet you, Jenny. Izzy and the kids talk about you every time they call."

I nodded politely and stood back, as far away as possible from a slathering dog and giggling girl rolling around on the floor. The emotion in this foyer was depressing. Hugs and kisses and back slaps and inside jokes. I felt like the man in the moon, just a shadow full of craters, looking down on a green and perfect planet from which I was estranged.

I wasn't the only one. Heath stood in the archway of the kitchen, obviously ill at ease, and feeling guilty that he was responsible for his father leaving his prized fieldwork.

Standing taller than Izzy or the children, both Heath and his father stared silently into each other's eyes. The urgency to touch, yet the restraint, was almost palpable.

The current was so strong that it was something I would not in my lifetime forget.

Heath seemed slow to move, as though gathering his thoughts from somewhere deep inside, somewhere he didn't want to go. His discomfort was painful to watch.

"Son?" The word was a question; the widespread arms were the answer. Heath moved along that imaginary line from stars in the Big Dipper to the Little Dipper toward True North straight into his father's arms and didn't move.

I walked through the open front door, past a pile of gear that Mr. Earnshaw had dropped, around to the pen where Pip waited; I pulled my only friend in the world into my lap and fought back tears.

Ten minutes later, Hareton settled next to me, giggling. Controlled, dry eyed and on the look out for that sharp-eared Anubis that might want to reclaim his pen, I said: "What's so funny, Hareton?"

"Dad is. He sent me to find you. He's cooking breakfast and then going to bed with Mom. He's been driving all night, said he was on the road already when she called him. He said after breakfast, we should all go entertain ourselves. He and Mom will make their own entertainment. That's his idea of being subtle. Old people like them. You'd think they'd get over it." Hareton ducked his head to hide flushed cheeks.

"Oh yeah. I told him you knew absolutely everything there is to know about math and geometry. You could answer any question. He said not likely since you're only fifteen. But, I bet him ten bucks that you could. Heath put ten dollars in the pot saying Dad will lose, so I'll get twenty if I win. Dad says we've got to come straight to the kitchen, no detours to the Internet."

"Can I, at least, hear the question?"

"Yep. What is the meaning of Q.E.D. and Q.E.F.?"

Always eager to show off, I tried not to act too impatient. Encouraging Hareton to bet wasn't a good idea. Aunt Izzy had told me how gambling addiction was a problem for some of her people.

I carefully looped the latch on the dog pen in case Raven didn't take well to a guest in his quarters. "What do I get if you're right?" I ruffled Hareton's spiky hair, careful not to take him into any octopus arms like Sue Ann did, though I really wanted to.

"Praise." He giggled again. "The satisfaction of being the queen bee of geometry." Hareton's rhyming made me think of Maylene and her goofy versifying. Those days at the Compound seemed far away. I was with interesting people now. Not a bigot or sadist in sight.

The air of happy expectation when Hareton and I walked into the kitchen seemed more in line with what I had come to expect of the Earnshaws than that bad business last night.

"Sorry, Jenny. Didn't mean to put you on the spot, but this son of mine taunted me. Forget the Latin. Just quote one of Euclid's definitions and I'll pay up—and give you a pile of my eggs and chorizo—brought the sausage all the way from New Mexico." Mr. Earnshaw's grin was almost identical to Heathcliff's.

"Q.E.D. *quod erat demonstratum*—which was shown to be proven; Q.E.F. *quod erat faciendum*—which was to be done. I'll take the eggs without the sausage. I'm not fond of rare sausage." The pinkish lumps in the eggs reminded me of the raw sausage I'd cooked for Mr. Darken, hoping above hope that he'd get deadly pork parasites.

"Bravo, Jenny! Just try the chorizo. The color comes from red pepper in it. You haven't lived until you've had chorizo for breakfast. Just as I tell my other kids. One bite. That's all. We're not a clean plate club around here."

I would have torn raw meat from a bone just to hear this jovial, welcoming man say "my other kids" and mean me.

The boisterous conversation around the breakfast table came to an abrupt halt when Mr. Earnshaw let something slip. "When I filled up the jeep just as I pulled onto the Res this morning, I saw Ebon Riley at the next pump. He was driving a big, black Cadillac. Said he got a good trade-in recently."

Heath and I stared at each other. He spoke first: "Gomer Darken has a black Cadillac. Jenny and I were sure that we spotted it behind that tall grass at the end of our cul-de-sac a couple of nights ago. It took off before I could see the driver, but he wasn't wearing a Stetson. Ebon always does. Covers his receding hairline." Heath snorted derisively as he pushed his fingers through his thick neck-length hair that had taken on a cinnamon hue.

"It *was* Mr. Darken's car. Hidden behind those ornamental grasses. He was watching this house." I tried to lower my voice to keep the fear I had been feeling at bay.

I didn't want to put a damper on this homecoming with my problems. The Earnshaws had a few of their own.

Heath plowed through his father's eggs and chorizo with the speed of a NASCAR driver, but there was a restive quality about him this morning, edgy, as though his thoughts were somewhere else. Maybe on Ebon and Sue Ann. The snide comment about Ebon's imminent baldness seemed out of character. Heath mercilessly teased his mother and Hareton, but he was never mean-spirited. Groundless as her accusations might be, Sue Ann had been part of Heath's life for years. Obviously, he was worried.

An uncomfortable silence settled around the table. My comment about someone in a Chrysler watching the house must have unnerved everyone. It was time for me to make an exit, do a run, clear my head, drum the ground with great, long strides—not those little pointy-toed shuffles that Sue Ann was doing last night, even if they did make her glimmer like a supernova.

"If no one minds, I'll let you have some family time together. I need to go for a run. I'm getting out of shape." I intercepted a glance that Heath shot his father.

"Do you mind having company, Jenny? I could use some exercise." Heath pushed back from the table. "We'll probably be gone for more than an hour. That back road toward the lake won't have much traffic this time of year."

# CHAPTER 16

After skirting down alleys, jogging past the deso-late grounds of the Tribal Center, and taking what Heath called a shortcut through someone's newly tilled garden, we trotted onto a gravel road pocked with craters. I kicked up the pace but watched the road. I'd be sur-prised if this road had any traffic. One of those pits could take out an axle.

Preparing for a 10-K was all business for me, no time for jogging along and chatting. That could happen when I had reached my tolerance for suffering. That's what run-ners learn to do, bit by bit, to increase speed. If I overdid it today, I could rest with Trollope and ice. I needed to keep my eyes on this pitted road, push myself, and ignore my left shin announcing a bit of tibial stress.

What I couldn't ignore were two very large, fresh skid marks. They formed a double track, then a second pair of tracks, crisscrossed by a third set—as though a car had stopped suddenly, backed up quickly, and sped forward again. Maybe avoiding a deer? Smashing into deer was a hazard of driving through these forests. The pattern of skids made odd obtuse angles.

Just in front of the last skid, the gravel bunched into an untidy mound with a wide scraped swath leading toward the firs lining the road. I stopped and looked behind me. Heath was more than a hundred yards back, huffing but gaining ground.

A suffering animal might need immediate attention. A wide trench bordered by bright green, leathery kinnickinnick, known as bear berry, leveled out onto the forest floor.

I saw the pale, still feet, perfect isosceles triangles, the kind of feet that the early Renaissance painter Piero put on his angels—T.S. Eliot called them "unoffending feet."

My breathing had become intolerably ragged, but I forced myself to move forward. The bundle rolled into the forest shrubbery might have a pulse, a beating heart.

She didn't. She had a broken heart. And a bloody tibia sticking up through the denim of her jeans like a stalk of one of those lilies that burst up at the end of summer—surprise lilies, naked ladies.

She had curled into a protective circle so that the left side of her flayed face pressed itself into the forest floor to conceal its horror of exposed flesh the color of liver.

I remember when bending over the cool, pale face of my friend Abigail, caressed by the fake polyester satin of her casket in Zion Chapel, that the effort had taken all the strength I could muster. But, I had done it for Abigail's mother and for the truth in a bruised neck.

Bending over this scooped-up, tossed aside bundle of a beautiful young girl who could never be put back together didn't take strength. It took a leap of courage that I never knew I had. Lifting in the morning breeze as though it had a life of its own, a single strand of ebony hair glistened like jet beads in the sunlight.

"What's over there, Jenny? What have you found?" Heath's voice soared into a register higher than Hareton's.

"Don't come over here! Stay back!" I retraced my steps back toward Heath who stood perspiring, his olive skin ashen with dread.

He ignored me, stepped a few feet forward and softly said: "My god." Then he threw up chorizo and eggs all over my Merrills. Before I could stop him, he dropped down, spread-eagled like Di Vinci's Vitruvian man, and clasped the only part of Sue Ann that remained pristine, pure. Her feet.

It wasn't a Native American chant that filled the space. Great, rasping sobs soared and then disappeared into arpeggios of sound, gravelly, like little mice feet.

Then Edward Lear moored him. "They sailed away for a year and a day to the land where the Bong-tree grows." He lifted a tear-stained face to me. "The Owl and the Pussycat. That was Sue Ann's favorite poem. Mom read it to us endlessly."

Heath stood abruptly, brushed clots of regurgitated chorizo off his pants and said: "When we die, we go to the edge of the end of living. And that's it, Jenny."

I was shocked and saddened, but I didn't really know Sue Ann. And, guiltily, didn't like what I knew about her. But in her native dress, under the canopy of stars last night, she looked like something so rare that the Hubble space telescope might have discovered a new galaxy and beamed it back to earth.

"I think this may be a crime scene, and we're messing it up." I held Heath's arm tightly and backed him up.

"Crime scene? What are you talking about? For some reason, Sue Ann must have walked down this road last night and been hit by a car. Maybe the person thought it was a deer and drove on."

"No." My rebuttal was more assured than I was feeling. "Look at the tire tracks. They stop, back up, start again and then head on toward the lake. Something is very wrong here. Do you want me to stay with Sue Ann while you go for help?" I didn't really want to be here with a body, but Heath's chest was heaving so hard that I feared to leave him.

"You're faster. The Tribal Police are next to the Council building. Flag down a car if you see one. Go! Go! This sucks, Jenny. This really sucks!"

I paced myself the way I would on the second half of a 10K, faster and faster, not even looking at the road. A pothole couldn't make my pain worse. Whether Heath grieved for a girl who might have been his lover or simply his childhood friend didn't matter. I grieved for his misery. It became my sorrow.

The resinous odor of fir and pine trees rose all about me as I ran. The morning sun turned them into a kaleidoscope of greens—a lush viridian and gentle cinnabar topped by pale green at the tips, screaming with life.

Suddenly, anger swept over me so fiercely that I pounded along at a world-record pace. This boundless, beautiful world should not contain such evil. Wicked people sully it; they blaspheme it. In Heath's terms. This sucks.

The blast of a horn that broke my stride and nearly caused me to fall also sucked. I halted my offending finger midair when I saw that it was Heath's father in his jeep.

He skidded to a stop and shouted: "Where's Heath, Jenny? We need you two to help. Sue Ann's missing. The last time she was seen was at the powwow last night. Her father is frantic with worry!"

As I climbed into the jeep, heaving from my fast run, I mulled over the verb "worry." Intransitive. No object. Sue Ann's father would soon be confronted with an object that would conclude his life as he knew it. That's what the death of someone we love does, marks a boundary and closes us in on ourselves. I couldn't bear to be the messenger.

"What's wrong, Jenny? You look ill. Why isn't Heath with you?"

"He's with her, with Sue Ann." Relief flooded his face but was immediately replaced by anxiety. "I thought after what Izzy said that they . . ."

"She's dead!" I interrupted, the words pealing harshly out of a throat that wanted to take them back, to make them not true.

Mr. Earnshaw rolled to a halt in the middle of the road, letting the jeep idle, as though he didn't trust himself to move an inch forward or speak a single word.

The messenger had to fill in the silent gap. "About two miles down that old road toward the lake, I found her.

Someone ran over her. Heath was behind me . . . I tried to get him not to . . . he came and saw . . . a terrible thing . . . and he was . . ." My self-absorbed sobbing strangled off rational speech. The memory of Heathcliff holding onto the perfectly symmetrical feet of Sue Ann and weeping into the earth overpowered my ability to think logically.

And then it didn't. The roar of the jeep and the sudden swing onto the old lake road made me screech. "You can't drive too far down that road. There are tire marks. They show how she was hit. It's a crime scene."

"Show me where to stop. I'm calling the Tribal Police now." He flipped open his phone, rolled through contacts, and punched a button. "This is Bill Earnshaw. My kids found Sue Ann. I don't think you should tell her father yet. It's bad. I'm about two miles out on the old lake road. Stop behind my jeep when you get there."

He listened quietly then retorted, "Behind my jeep. I know you are in charge."

"Here!" I shouted. "No further. You can see Heath just beyond the edge of the road, sitting in the bushes. The skid marks start about forty feet back from him."

Instead of slamming on the brakes and rushing to his son as I thought he would do, Mr. Earnshaw slowed down carefully, pulled onto the side of the road, and took a big camera out of his glove compartment. "I need to take photographs of the road before Buddy Yalseh shows up. He was on dispatch. A junior officer and full of himself. Says he'll decide where to park. The idiot." He focused an oversized lens on the tracks and began taking shots from different angles.

# CHAPTER 17

When Buddy Yalseh roared up in a Dodge pickup, swerved around the jeep and skidded halfway through the tire marks ahead, he wiped out most of the evidence. By threshing through the low shrubbery near Sue Ann's body, he managed to eliminate traces of any possible footprints that Heath and I had been careful to avoid.

Out of the corner of my eye, I watched Mr. Earnshaw step carefully between the tracks, bend over and scoop up bits of gravel with a plastic spoon that he sealed into small bags. He dropped them in his camera bag and sent a warning look toward Buddy Yalseh. "Don't touch her body until the doctor gets here. You've already hashed the scene."

The circus-parade anticipation on Buddy Yalseh's gleaming, puffy face blanched when he leveraged his boot against her head and brusquely turned Sue Ann's face toward the bright sun.

Sue Ann was in desperate need of the Phantom of the Opera's mask to extend past the left side of her face and hide the dark crimson meningeal hemorrhage. That's when Heath came to her aid.

The first punch flattened Buddy. The second one stopped midway as Mr. Earnshaw grabbed his son's arm and steered him toward the jeep. "Sue Ann's gone, son. Don't take it out on Buddy."

He yanked Buddy to his feet, brushed off his jacket while keeping an ironbound grip on his arm. "You can tell Sam I got good photos of the tracks where she was hit. I also got some glass from the site. You need to watch where you put your boots, Buddy. Sue Ann's father would do more than just punch you for such disrespect."

Buddy's boots had done more than demonstrate disrespect for a corpse. They had made shambles of a crime scene. I looked back at him rubbing his jaw and glaring balefully in our direction as Mr. Earnshaw hustled Heath and me into his jeep.

No one spoke during the ride home. Aunt Izzy stood on the porch, her face as swollen as though she had encountered a swarm of angry wasps. "Sue Ann's father is at the Tribal Police office. Sam said he'd like to see you now. He'll be here later to talk to Heath and Jenny." Aunt Izzy looped an arm around Heath casually, ignoring the fact that his puffy eyes were a mirror image of her own.

"Sam Wilson, Jenny. He's the chief of police. Just routine questions. This happened on the Res. The Tribal Police will handle things. No need to worry."

Last words fascinate me. Oscar Wilde's comment about the tacky wallpaper. Brautigan's "Messy, isn't it?"

Aunt Izzy's "no need to worry" prompted me to worry about everything.

Why would someone deliberately run down Sue Ann? Why had she been walking alone at night on that particular road? Who might not have an alibi for the time she was killed?

Heath. After his argument with his mother last night, he tore out in his jeep. I had no idea where he'd been. I assumed that his parents knew. They seemed reconciled and good-spirited earlier around the breakfast table.

THE THREE MEN banging on the front door didn't appear good-spirited in the least. One was Buddy Yalsey, tracking mud like animal spore across Aunt Izzy's Navajo rug in the foyer. Looming half a head taller over Buddy was a man who must be the Chief of Police. He wore a weatherproof brown jacket like Buddy's. His baseball cap said: Idaho Spuds. The face under it was grim as he lock stepped a man who must be Sue Ann's father into the house.

Staring pointedly at Buddy's feet, Aunt Izzy said: "Come into the kitchen. We can sit at the table there. I'll make coffee." She pulled me next to her. "Chief Wilson, Carl Snelling, this is Jenny. She came upon . . . when she was running . . . she and Heath." Aunt Izzy was having a hard time saying Sue Ann's name.

Not surprising. A chasm had opened behind the black eyes flickering with despair in Mr. Snelling's gaunt, grayish face. He looked like one of those old sepia Curtis prints of a forlorn Indian chief trying to make the camera see him as noble. This man was savage in his grief.

Buddy plopped onto a kitchen chair and looked hopefully toward the coffeepot. Chief Wilson shoved back a chair for Mr. Snelling who backed against the wall, cocked out his elbows as though he held an invisible rifle and fired—at Heath.

"She tell you she was pregnant, you good-for-nothing-piece of shit! You take her out like road kill. You do that to my little girl."

Mr. Snelling wasn't asking questions; he was making an awful noise, like a road grader repeatedly scraping concrete. The judge and jury had convened in Aunt Izzy's kitchen. If this were tribal police procedure, I'd rather be convicted in Texas.

Standing with his back against Aunt Izzy's big Aga stove, Heathcliff flinched repeatedly, like one of those hooded traitors waiting for the fatal bullet from the firing squad.

It came from another quarter. "Not another word, Carl. Not in my home. I can't imagine the grief you are feeling. I can only know what we feel for the loss of Sue Ann who was like our own child. This isn't helping the police find who killed her."

Mr. Earnshaw's voice was resonant as a hymn. He didn't mince words. The word "killed" rolled out like acid and actually cut the tension in the room.

Then a glacial chill fell. The next ice age seemed imminent as I heard my name called out.

"Jenny, Izzy told me that you saw Sue Ann last night in the women's bathroom at the Council Building. You talked to her. Then you and Heath went on a run this morning and found her. I'd like for you to tell me anything that would be helpful to us—as precisely as you can."

Chief Wilson's deadpan manner was so much like Joe Friday from the old TV Dragnet series that I almost smiled. I felt an immediate kinship with this man who still wore his Idaho Spuds baseball cap inside the house. I was nothing if not precise.

Within a few minutes, I had summarized the scene in the bathroom but modified the description of Sue Ann heaving over the toilet. Respect for the dead required leaving out messy details. I left out even more details about her mangled body out of concern for her father. The ambulance had transported her to the hospital in Coeur d'Alene. He'd know too much too soon.

I did give exact times: when we left the house, why I stopped to look at the tire tracks on the road, and how I purposefully walked into the shrubbery.

"And why was that little lady? Looking for something you already knew was there? Something Heath, here, told you about? Something you planned on hiding?" Buddy Yalseh's rude comment hung like a bad odor in the air.

"No, Mr. Yalseh. From the patterns of the skid marks, my first impression was that someone had hit an animal, maybe a deer. I thought it might be hurt, still alive."

I couldn't let it go after his implication about Heath. I could draw blood too. "In spite of Mr. Earnshaw's caution, you drove right through the skid marks; you tromped through where the Bear Berry bushes had been smashed down; what you did to . . ."

"I think Chief Wilson gets the picture, Jenny. What's done is done. You gave a very detailed account." Mr. Earnshaw patted my back insistently, the way my mother used to when my mouth couldn't quit flapping.

Mr. Snelling opened his again, still glaring across the room at Heath. "I'm still waiting for an explanation of where you were last night, Heath. Buddy here," he clapped the deputy on the back, "says he saw you tearing out of town in that old jeep of yours around ten o'clock, heading toward the east highway."

Bill Earnshaw nodded at his son, stricken with silence. "Tell them, son. Tell them what you told me."

Heathcliff might have been a zombie, one of those resurrected corpses with a ghastly pallor and no connection to the living. His words were those of an automaton, set to run until someone flipped the stop switch. "Sue Ann came by to get me to help set up the tables for last night. That's what she said. She really wanted to tell me that she was pregnant, maybe three months. She wasn't sure. She said we should get married, and things would be OK."

Aunt Izzy moved over next to him and clutched his hand. "Sue Ann knew that I wasn't the father. I couldn't have been. She said I should help her as a friend. If it didn't work out then we'd go our own ways. I told her I couldn't do that."

Mr. Snelling sat shaking his head skeptically; his expression suggested that was exactly what Heath should have done. "You'll have the test done. No getting around that, boy."

Aunt Izzy swung around to face him, linked arm in arm with her son as though absolutely assured that no test would incriminate Heath.

"Go on, Heath. Tell us anything you remember at the powwow that would help us. Then, we need to know exactly when you left home and what you were doing last night." Chief Wilson's tone was flat, as though he knew he had been following a false lead.

"I was upset about what Sue Ann said. We didn't argue. I just told her I wouldn't go along with her plans. Then I played the drums. She danced. I didn't see her again." Heath moved slightly apart from his mother.

"When we got home from the powwow, Mom told me that Sue Ann said she was pregnant, and I was the father. We argued. That's when I went to the Compound to try to see Josh Barnes."

"Anybody there that can verify that? I didn't know they let nonbelievers inside." Buddy snickered then gasped as Chief Wilson gave his shin a whack with the tip of his boot.

"Mrs. Barnes can verify that I was there. I got in through a place over the fence where Josh and I used to go. I knew the guards wouldn't let me inside the gates. They're armed with Uzis now. I went past the barn and through the big privet hedge that cordons off the Barnes's house."

I nodded. I remembered that privet hedge. Lorena was playing with some children just on the other side of it the last time I saw her.

Heath glanced over at me with a warning in his eyes. I was the Earnshaw niece and cousin. No need to complicate things by revealing what I knew about the Compound layout.

"Josh wasn't at home. His mom said they still keep him locked up at night in that place where single men live. I visited with Mrs. Barnes for a couple of hours."

"Hoo, boy! You think we believe you talked to somebody's mother for two hours—the same night your girlfriend got run over?" Buddy guffawed at his own insight, then shot a glance around the table to see if anyone else was amused. Chief Wilson clearly was not.

"Go ahead, Heath. Sorry about the interruption."

Heath paused as though not sure how much he wanted to reveal about his visit with Mrs. Barnes. "The time went fast. I hadn't seen Josh's mom for a year. We were catching up. It was past midnight when I left. I had to cut back through the horse pasture to get to my jeep. I think it must have been around one o'clock when I got home. As I came down the hall, I could see Jenny's door partway open. Mom was sleeping in there with Jenny. Cathy and Hareton were in their bedrooms upstairs."

Heath casually, but purposefully, gave all of us alibis for the time that might be of most interest to the tribal police. He was careful not to reveal anything about his visit with Mrs. Barnes. That's the information I was dying to hear.

*Dying.* We use that word incorrectly and casually when we really mean longing or yearning. For some reason, I thought of the war dead. Six million. Gas ovens. Hiroshima. Deaths beyond comprehension. Those deaths were an abstraction, in multiples too unreal to be real.

After my confinement with the Bible at the Winner house, I had been giving some thought to the Father, the Son, and the Holy Ghost. Two gods and a phantom up there somewhere should be taking better care of the flock.

Like one of those firmly aligned, breakaway Russian countries—Belarus or the Ukraine—the Earnshaw family with me in the center moved like a block behind the Chief and Mr. Snelling to the front porch.

"Either get in the car or walk, Buddy!" The Chief's patience seemed to be wearing thin as he watched Buddy sniffing around the jeeps of Heath and his father like a dog on point.

Like Anubis sniffing out a new corpse for the afterlife, Raven stalked Buddy until he jumped inside the car and slammed the door. Then, Raven's ears perked up; a fierce growl sounded deep down in his throat as he charged the dog pen, sailing right over the latched gate.

With a squeal and a shudder, Pip slunk into the lowest form of submission possible. He was my dog for sure. Giving up and rolling over without so much as a growl in return.

Back in the kitchen, I wanted to say something in Heath's defense, to finger Ebon Riley as a possible father of Sue Ann's baby, but it had been easier to remain silent in the face of Mr. Snelling's anger and grief. I knew that when the fury had burned itself out, there would be only ash where Mr. Snelling's soul had been.

Aunt Izzy had echoed my thoughts as Mr. Snelling and Chief Wilson were leaving. "He survived his wife's death because he had Sue Ann. He won't try for life again." She dabbed her eyes with a dishtowel. "He has nothing left but revenge—and Heath seems to be in his sights."

After I untangled Pip from Raven's jaws, ignoring Hareton's "that's just the way dogs play, Jenny," I put him on a leash and decided I'd go check on Mr. Tomeh's onion shoots. The least I could do was water them while he searched the streets of Portland for his brother.

At the corner of the house, Aunt Izzy, Heath, and Mr. Earnshaw stood arm in arm like a plotting cabal. I overhead Heath say something about Josh's mother and Elder Grund that sent Aunt Izzy's face aflame. Then, I heard my name and something about my uncle. I flushed and backed away. My appetite for eavesdropping was waning.

Why would Mrs. Barnes have anything to do with that doddering old so-called electrician in the Compound? Considering the way that he linked cheap extension cords together in violation of every electrical code, he'd probably be zapped before that stent for his heart could do its job.

The grudge I held Elder Grund dripped with the constancy of bile from my liver. It was his interference that stopped my grand electrification of the Compound gates and probably a universal grilling of its elders. Why would the Earnshaws be discussing me in the same conversation about him? Time for a long walk with Pip.

# CHAPTER 18

Three days later, I walked into a Catholic church with the Earnshaw family. "We'll sit near the back," Aunt Izzy whispered. "Pay our respects and leave. I don't want to go to the gravesite. I can't bear seeing Sue Ann put into the ground."

"We have to, Izzy. If not for Carl, then for Sue Ann and the memory of her mother," Mr. Earnshaw whispered back. "We already settled this."

We had. On the morning of the funeral, Heath came down to breakfast in ragged jeans and a tee shirt and announced: "I don't believe in funerals. We should do like the Plains tribes did years ago, just put the remains up on a platform for the birds to eat."

"That's crass, Heath." His father's voice was brusque. "Funerals are for the living. For thousands of years, humans have honored their dead. As a would-be archeologist, you should know that—and appreciate it."

He shifted his chair closer to Heath. "I know this is hard for you, son. You've been hearing all the gossip. You know that Chief Wilson hasn't a clue about what happened on that road or why. He'll figure it out sooner

LAND OF THE BONG TREE

or later. He usually does. In the meantime, this family is going as a unit to Sue Ann's funeral."

He raised one eyebrow at me, still in a pair of Hareton's old pajamas. "That means you, too, Jenny. Izzy found you some shoes so you don't have to wear tennis shoes. Heath. Get it together—suit, tie, the works. It's going to be a difficult day. We'll get through it better just by being with each other."

As a spectator and not a participant, my second Catholic funeral left me dry-eyed and curious. At my father's funeral with half a dozen onlookers, the priest's perfunctory words over a gleaming casket left me focused on only two things: the fake grass hiding a raw wound in the ground and Mother's casual announcement that my father had a brother—an uncle I never knew existed.

THE CHURCH OVERFLOWED with floral tributes—and people packed stem to stern in every pew. Folding chairs lined the back and side aisles. Battling the spicy odor of incense, great bunches of hothouse flowers sent up the stale perfume of refrigerated blooms. An organ whiffled out "Ave Maria" as mourners tiptoed into the church, whispering in voices too low for the dead to hear.

Five Earnshaws and one Hatchet scrunched hip to hip on a back pew into a space designed for four.

A shiny, pale pink casket with the lid battened down held place of honor adjacent to the center aisle. Sue Ann's father stumbled toward the front of the church with what

I assumed to be Sue Ann's aunts, uncles, and cousins clustered around him.

An honor guard of priests and altar boys, one armed with a swinging thurible wafting incense, paraded down the center aisle to the front of the church. At that moment, I could feel Heath's smothered sobs shaking his body.

I might have comforted him, but I thought I'd better keep my hands to myself. So, I thought about how Buddhism explains bad Karma—that good can come from bad things happening to good people. That always seemed a bit far-fetched to me, especially as I stared at Sue Ann's bier.

The priest looked dolefully down at Sue Ann's father and said something about two sparrows being sold for a farthing and how "not one of them falls to the ground apart from your Father."

That made me think about the Trinity again—Father, Son, and Holy Ghost—and how in the name of logic could they poke around in the human sphere to prevent human and vehicle collisions? With over 110 million trucks in the USA, how could that Holy Ghost phantom have prevented my father from missing a curve and ending up in the McKenzie River? With over 250 million cars on the road, how could the three holies keep a lone girl on a country road safe from an angry driver?

The piercing falsetto of a woman who seemed to be wearing an ill-fitting orangish toupee stopped my thoughts in their tracks so to speak. "We shall sleep, but not forever; there will be a glorious dawn; we shall meet, to part, no, no never, on the resurrection morn!" She sang on and on through verse after verse, so bad that my weird stepmother Maylene might have penned them.

Sue Ann deserved better. A girl whirling away the last hours of her life under a starry sky in a spangled dress deserved better music at her funeral. So, I gave it to her. In my mind. Only in my thoughts.

Bobby Dylan sang "Hey, Mr. Tambourine Man, play a song for me; in this jingle jangle morning, I'll come following you." I mentally went through every word with Bobby's sultry, matter-of-fact, mumbling lyrics ringing in my head.

I was just ending the next to the last verse "let me forget about today until tomorrow" when a sharp elbow jabbed my ribs. Heath lifted a single eyebrow and then smiled companionably at me as though he might be hearing Bobby in my head.

A Tribal Police Honor Guard orchestrated the procession to the graveyard: the hearse, the funeral home limo with Mr. Snelling, and a lineup of cars with their lights on. The six of us crammed into Mr. Earnshaw's jeep, waiting until the last car had pulled out of the church parking lot.

"Izzy? Bill?" Chief Wilson stuck his head into the window on Aunt Izzy's side. "I need a word with Heath before you leave."

Sitting in the backseat between Hareton and Heath, I could feel Heath's body suddenly tense, preparing for some kind of blow. "Just say what you need to say to all of us, Chief. Our family doesn't have secrets." His voice was so low that I wasn't sure it carried past my ear.

The Chief's did. Like a boom box splintering the funereal quiet of the almost-vacant parking lot, he said: "Lab report came back this morning. You're not the one, Heath. I believed what you said, but we have to follow every lead. Can't say we have one now."

I was just about to offer Chief Wilson a clue when I felt a pinch on my arm as fierce as a scorpion's sting. In unison, all four windows of the jeep mechanically rolled up against my protest.

As Mr. Earnshaw pulled out of the parking lot behind the last car in the journey to the graveyard, Aunt Izzy turned around and said softly. "I know you mean to help, Jenny, but it isn't our way to accuse any tribal member. Mr. Snelling's accusations against Heath were those of a grieving father. We can forgive him. We simply have to let the Tribal Police do their work. We can answer their questions, but they have to ask them first."

Considering the accusations against Heath and a paternity test in the face of his repeated denials, I was still on the side of Shylock. I'd want a pound of flesh—probably from that creepy Buddy who had been whacking the bumper on Heath's old jeep that morning he came to call with the Chief and Sue Ann's father.

I twisted slightly so that I could observe Heath's profile as he stared fixedly at the ditches filled with early spring flowers alongside the highway. Heath might have been admiring the pale pink bitterroot clumped along the way. *Lewisa rediviva* It was named for Meriwether Lewis who ate the root and pronounced it bitter. Aunt Izzy told me that it made a fine soup after the first boiling was dumped.

Bitterroot. Not getting to the root of something evil. That was bitter. My tongue tasted sour. Being shushed—even as politely as Aunt Izzy had put a sock in my mouth—went against the grain of me.

I didn't like Ebon Riley. I didn't the way he looked at me. I remembered him standing near the Tribal Council building covertly watching Sue Ann as she talked to Aunt Izzy. Presumably, no one saw her after she walked away. Someone had. She didn't go on a deserted road at night, all alone.

Aware of his leg pressed against mine, I turned my attention to Heath's perfectly sculpted profile again. Sometimes, when Heath was too near, as he was in this crowded jeep, I felt if I opened my mouth that adjectives would spew out like words from a trashy romance: foxy, breathtaking, hot, sensuous.

A leg on the other side pressed against me and Hareton squeaked: "My math teacher said that Euclid hog-tied geometry. How do you explain that, Jenny?"

I did. All the way to the graveyard. That place could have used geometric oversight. Lines of stones flexed at odd angles; paths that should have been straight zigzagged.

The cluster of mourners around the vile green of fake grass formed an equilateral triangle with Sue Ann's pink casket suspended at the point. I reluctantly trailed the Earnshaw family. That sham grass trying to hide the newly trenched hole took me back to my father's gravesite in Portland. I didn't want to remember.

Cautiously, we all hung back, as far away from the grave as possible without attracting attention. What did attract my attention was an eerie chorus of wailing from black-clad women standing by the grave. The piercing laments sent chills up my spine.

"It's the old way, Jenny. Keening. The older women in the tribe still do it at the gravesite. It's not acceptable in church. But here, outside, in this place, it sends up a message of loss." Aunt Izzy had remained dry-eyed during the funeral. Now, tears flooded down her cheeks. I joined her in weeping for Sue Ann—or maybe for those wailing women who thought that someone up in heaven could hear them.

"BILL AND I have been talking, Jenny, about your . . . your . . . situation." Aunt Izzy looked across the dinner table with a kind of hopefulness I welcomed. An erstwhile daughter and sister, I had left my mother and Lorena with the Compound perverts and felt a terrible urgency to redeem myself.

Between the drama of the funeral and the clearing of Heath's name, I was beginning to feel that my own, increasingly present, worries were being put on the back burner while the Earnshaws dealt with their own problems.

"Heath told us quite a bit about his conversation with Mrs. Barnes. She and Josh are virtual prisoners in the

Compound. Elders Winner and Bonner have threatened to send Josh to another ward down by Boise if his mother proves troublesome."

"Troublesome?" I echoed. *A quiet, retiring woman who bakes pottery in her kiln?*

"One of the elders, a Mr. Grund hasn't been well lately. Something with his heart. Both of his wives are elderly and can't properly care for him." Aunt Izzy's lips thinned as though she had just tasted something bitter. "The elders may force Mrs. Barnes to go through one of those celestial marriages they arrange so cavalierly—with that old man."

I nodded emphatically. I knew all about celestial marriages. I had watched my mother being "bound for eternity" to that warthog Mr. Darken.

"That kind of marriage isn't legal, but Mrs. Barnes is afraid that Josh will do something out of anger, something that will put him at risk. When a widow is taken in marriage, all of her property goes to the husband. Their home and their land that should legally go to Josh will be Mr. Grund's."

"The incompetent electrician," I interjected. "I know him. He's the skinflint that stuck his nose in my business. I had talked Mr. Darken into buying electrical supplies and batteries to fix the fence—actually, I was planning to electrify the front gates like a firework show. Elders would have flared out of both ends like Roman candles."

I shoveled in another mouthful of Aunt Izzy's taco salad—a concoction of ground beef, beans, cheese, onions, tomatoes and avocados on a mound of lettuce and cilantro. "By the way, Aunt Izzy. I fixed both those sockets on the lamps by the sofa."

An uneasy pall settled over the table as five forks lowered simultaneously.

I giggled. It was the first laughter in the room since we had left Sue Ann stranded above an open pit with fake grass beneath the straps holding her casket in midair as though it might just travel on down the road and not into the ground.

"Don't worry. I know what I'm doing. The sockets were loose on those antique lamps; I stripped part of that old, fuzzy cord and reconnected the wires. You need to get rid of that old cord. If you like that look, they still make that old style of cord. I can replace all of it, including the plugs. Unless you're worried about pyrotechnics."

"What Izzy and I are worried about, Jenny, doesn't have a thing to do with your skills as an electrician. It's about how we can help your mother, your sister, Mrs. Barnes and Josh get way from the CPRC. Our Tribal Police have no authority off the Reservation." Mr. Earnshaw pushed back his chair and dropped his chin on his hand just like Rodin's thinker, frozen in bronze.

"For Christ's sake, Dad. This is the U.S. of A. Fanatics can't keep people against their will. They can't take property that isn't legally theirs!"

Heath had been in a brown study since we left the graveyard. His outburst lifted my spirits. He was right.

"You weren't born when the ATF and FBI raided the Branch Davidians' ranch near Waco. It's been twenty years, but memories are long. That fiasco cost the lives of 86 men, women and children. It's unlikely that the feds will tangle with a group like CPRC. They live quietly. They don't engage in obvious criminal activity," Mr. Earnshaw added resignedly.

"Putting their CPA in a bullpen. Bigamy. Forced marriages to underage girls. Breaking their necks when they resist." The rancor in my words reddened Mr. Earnshaw's face. An image of Abigail's bruised neck tucked into the satin rosettes of her coffin got between my taco salad and me. I pushed back my chair, nauseated by the direction this conversation was heading.

"We know all that, Jenny. Bill is just pointing out the fact that we can't rely on federal officials to help. And, we probably shouldn't trust county law enforcement. Some of them might be on the CPRC payroll."

"You're leaving out the biggest fly in the ointment, Ma." Heath smiled wickedly in her direction. "Some on our Tribal Council are thick as thieves with the CPRC elders."

As though she knew exactly what he meant, Aunt Izzy dismissed his accusation. "The tribe and CPRC have profited mutually from grazing rights and leveraging contracts for livestock and grain. Josh's father was instrumental in setting up some of those enterprises."

"Izzy, you know as well as I do that Sam Barnes advised the Tribal Council in writing to end those agreements. Healthy business dealings are one thing. Tax evasion quite another." Mr. Earnshaw looked at me soberly. "I agree with Jenny—though I might not put it as bluntly. The law should have investigated Sam's death."

"His death and that of Jenny's friend Abigail for starters. Kidnapping, trafficking in underage girls, parading around wearing Uzis, and who knows what other crimes," Heath interrupted, pushed back his chair and assumed the same thinker's pose as his father.

They resembled two meditating bookends. The CPRC crimes of the past weren't my main concern. What might be happening to Mother and Lorena was foremost in my mind—with a nice warm corner of it left to worry about Josh.

As though she were reading my thoughts, Aunt Izzy turned to me and said brightly: "That's why Bill and I decided that you need to find this uncle of yours—the one you didn't know existed until your father died."

"But why would . . . I don't know why my father didn't . . . or why Mother let it slip at his funeral . . ." The muddle of my words didn't explain the grudge I'd had against my mysterious uncle from the moment Mother mentioned quite casually by my father's open grave that "your father's brother should be here." I didn't know if she meant as an onlooker or in my father's stead in the casket.

Five very curious Earnshaw faces watched me try to explain a non-uncle. Before my father died, we had one of those legally sealed-in families—two parents, two children, grandparents dead on both sides, nothing dangling off the family tree but a single branch—us. Father loving my mother to excess. Mother loving shopping to excess. Lorena and I dutifully filling in the spaces.

I thought of the only other comment that Mother had made about my uncle that day in the Compound when she told me to try to escape. She thought he might be a fisherman on the Oregon Coast. Sometimes I envisioned my elusive uncle hauling out salmon, tuna, halibut, and the prehistoric ling cod with rows of sharp teeth.

Other images crowded out the mundane ones. Sometimes he bobbed up and down in the waves like a toy duck in a bathtub. Or one of those homemade Dunkirk boats pulling wounded British soldiers out of the briny.

"More taco salad, Jenny?" Aunt Izzy pushed over a washtub-sized bowl to me. "We've decided to let you and Heathcliff and Hareton take a little trip to the coast to look for your uncle."

She picked up a credit card from the end of the kitchen counter and handed it to me. "I almost forgot. I set up your account, as we discussed. From the diamond."

"You keep your money, Jenny. The trip is our treat. Heath can drive Izzy's car. It's too far for a single day of driving. You can stay outside of Portland tomorrow and get to Charleston early the next day," Mr. Earnshaw chimed in. "Hareton will go with you."

"Charleston?" I asked, only faintly recalling it when I was searching the net to look for an elusive uncle.

Cathy's questions didn't have anything to do with finding a missing uncle. "It's not fair! Why does Hareton get to go and not me? Jenny's my special friend. Not his!"

Cathy's dad reached over and swung her out of her chair onto his lap and nuzzled her hair, the same way my father used to do. I might have wept with the remembrance, but I was too busy trying to think of why I shouldn't be on the road with the Earnshaw boys looking for an uncle who might not exist.

Aunt Izzy furnished me a reason. "It's been a terrible week for all of us. The shock of finding Sue Ann like that—and the accusation." She didn't mention Heath, but we all knew the toll it had taken on him. "Bill and I thought a little trip to the Oregon Coast would be a nice break for you kids. Hareton will be your chaperone. We don't want to give Mrs. Masset anything else to gossip about."

Hareton's chest expanded like a pouter pigeon. Heath looked perplexed. His father flung an arm across his shoulders. "I have a friend in the Oregon Department of Fish and Wildlife. I asked him if he had heard of fisherman named Hal Hatchet. I think you said that's his name, Jenny?"

I nodded, wondering if that seedy looking website for Hal's Holiday Fishing Charters I'd seen on Aunt Izzy's iMac had anything to do with my blood relative.

"My friend says everyone knows Hal. He's a fixture on the coast. Runs a few charters but mostly commercial fishing. I have his address in Charleston."

He turned toward Heath. "It's an easy route, Heath. Head from here to Spokane, then Portland and pick up the 101 to go south. Charleston's adjacent to Coos Bay."

I sunk lower and lower in my chair. Someone else was planning my future with an uncle who didn't know I existed. I couldn't retrieve my own mother and sister. I had nothing if the Earnshaws were giving me away to a stranger.

"I have to take care of Pip," my voice soared above the travel directions. "He needs me."

"I need you, Jenny. We all need you." Aunt Izzy's voice was as clear and soothing as gelatinous drops of aloe vera onto burned skin. "Because you're underage and we're not legally your guardians, we thought that if we can find your uncle, he might be willing to help us get your mother and sister."

"And Josh? And his mother?" Heath's voice soared into a higher register than Hareton's.

"Yes." Mr. Earnshaw's answer was decisive. "I have no intention of leaving my friend's son and wife in that miserable place. We just have to be creative about how we get them out of there. We're not exactly equipped to go up against Uzis."

Mr. Earnshaw reached for my hand. "I don't have a phone number for your uncle, Jenny. I didn't think it was my business to call him. We can try to locate a number, or you can just surprise him. However it works out. The Oregon Coast is gorgeous. Izzy booked a motel just south of Portland. We don't want you driving all the way without stopping."

A nondescript black duffle was on my bed. I immediately thought about that tacky Barbie roller bag that Mr. Darken had bought for my birthday and how I had packed it with my tools and old clocks and no clothes because I knew we wouldn't be staying.

For this trip, I threw in an extra top, Hareton's tacky PJs, and a couple of the butt clinging skirts. Might as well make an impression on this phantom uncle.

# CHAPTER 19

Annoyed at being alone in the back seat of Aunt Izzy's Honda, Hareton kept up a nonstop dialogue with himself to the outskirts of Portland. "I've thought of a game we can play to make the time pass, Jenny. It's called 'Famous Uncles.' I think I'll patent it."

"Put a sock in it, Hareton. Jenny is probably uneasy about meeting her uncle. You don't need to increase her anxiety." Heath flipped on the radio to a country music station playing Toby Keith.

"Oh, he ain't worth missing/Oh, we should be kissing/Stop all this foolish wishing."

I turned and rolled my eyes at Hareton in the backseat. If only Maylene could strum a guitar, she might make it in Nashville. She could slaughter rhyme as well as Toby could.

Heath got the message and flipped off the radio.

"Here's the way my famous uncle game goes. I'll go first to give you some good examples. There's the *Secret Garden*. The orphan Mary comes from India to a mansion in England where she meets a strange uncle and an even odder cousin—who may or may not be a hunchback."

"OK, Hareton. What is your point?" Heath asked in an irritated voice.

"The point is famous uncles, dummy. Now the next one is this—one of Mom's favorites. I'll give you the clue; you guess the uncle. The main character is not an orphan but gets sent from her own large family to live with her wealthy aunt and uncle and four cousins to improve her life. Her uncle has become wealthy off slaves working his property in Barbados. Who is he?"

Heath flipped on the radio again, obviously not a fan of Jane Austen. I decided to play Hareton's game. "*Mansfield Park*. Fanny's uncle is Lord Bertram."

"That was too easy. You give me one now, Jenny."

I thought about really wicked uncles in literature. They were legion. "OK. I'll give you an easy one. This uncle killed his brother, the king, married the queen, and plotted to get rid of his nephew—who, by the way, wanted to kill his uncle but couldn't seem to talk himself into it."

"Well. It's not Jane Austen. She doesn't kill anyone off. They just die of natural causes. It could be an English or French novel. They have lots of kings and queens. I give up. Too hard."

"*Hamlet*. The uncle was Claudius—a villain. His nephew had a chance to kill him while he prayed but knew his soul might go right up to heaven if he died while praying. Missed the opportunity and brought about his own death."

"I wonder if your uncle could be a villain." Hareton mused aloud.

"Hareton. I'm going to turn this car around right now and take you home if you don't quit harassing Jenny." Heath flipped on the radio again.

Lucinda Williams sang "Born to be Loved" in that elegant, gravelly voice of hers, and, blissfully, put Hareton to sleep.

I thought about his question. Could my uncle be a villain? Is that why my father never mentioned him? Is that why my mother offered only the vague possibility that he "might be a fisherman" and never mentioned him again?

We had photos of Mother's parents—and an endless log of her growing up, doted upon by her aging parents who, in their mid forties, appeared stunned to have a child. Not a single photograph from my father's side. It was as though he didn't come into existence until he emerged like a newborn chick in his 1995 wedding photo and couldn't quit smiling at the camera.

Maybe this mysterious brother of my father was like the red and hairy Esau who sold his birthright to Jacob for a pot of stew. It couldn't have been much of an estate that caused their estrangement. My father told me that he grew up poor and that his parents died when he was seventeen. He said he didn't like to "dwell on it." Whatever "it" meant. So he didn't.

"Jenny, don't let Hareton's silly games upset you," Heath patted my shoulder gently as he broke the speed limit zooming around a truck. "We'll find your uncle. They don't call us the Discovered People for no reason."

"The Discovered People?" I questioned, startled out of my reverie.

"Or Those Who Are Found Here, if you want a better translation. Hunting is in our blood. We roamed over four million acres before the feds stuck us on a fraction of what was originally our land." Heath's cavalier tone belied the vexation I suspected he felt.

"OK, great hunter," I responded, trying to match Heath's nonchalant attitude. "See if you can find our motel. I'm really sleepy."

WHEN I WOKE, Etta James was singing "I'll be seeing you in all the old familiar places," and I wanted to go somewhere to be sad by myself. I thought about how women singers and women writers understand grief so well. George Eliot knew the pervasive nature of grief. *She was no longer wrestling with the grief, but could sit down with it as a lasting companion and make it a sharer in her thoughts.*

I glanced over at Heath who kept his eyes glued to the road now that we were getting into heavy afternoon traffic in Portland. I wondered if Mr. Tomeh had found his brother, the other Mr. Tomeh by our old apartment. I was tempted to ask Heath to make a detour, but I didn't want him to see the squalor of our old neighborhood.

"Keep your eye out for the Holiday Inn Express. Mom booked us a room with two queens."

"I get the one with Jenny," a yawning Hareton woke up just enough to be offensive before he dropped off to sleep again.

Heath turned and gave me an obscene wink to let me know that Hareton wasn't the only one with sleeping arrangements on his mind. I watched his neck throb with just a mere pulsation. My fingertips could feel it even though they were curled harmlessly in my lap.

I was beginning to feel like one of those characters in an Edith Wharton novel, longing but not acting, feeling an invisible current between Heath and me but never grounding it in touch. Characters from novels popped into my thoughts often these days. Must be Aunt Izzy's influence.

To divert myself from improper thoughts, I fished around in my purse for the book of Donne's poems that Aunt Izzy had told me I'd like. I flipped it open: "Our hands were firmly cemented/By a fast balm, which thence did spring/Our eye-beams twisted, and did thread/Our eyes upon one double string."

The great sermonizer hit the nail on the head. He expressed eloquently what I was thinking in crass terms.

"I brought Bukowski's *The Pleasure of the Dammed*. Ma can't stand his poetry. I've identified with it lately. What book did she foist off on you? Jane or Charlotte or Emily?"

"There it is! There! On the left side! And fast food places thicker than mushrooms after a rain!"

"Your mother told us to eat healthy food, Hareton. Not go to a junk food place," I repeated Aunt Izzy's caution as I remembered the Pizza Hut on Powell Street where my father often took us for a weekend treat before we raided the used bookstore. "I have an idea. Let's check into the motel before it gets any darker and order pizza to be delivered. That way, we're not *going* to a junk food place."

"Great idea, Jenny! I have another uncle for you to guess."

Energized from his nap, Hareton hung halfway over the front seat and gave Heath unwanted directions and me his clues. "This uncle cut the cajones off his niece's boyfriend because he was so pissed at him for getting her pregnant. They called the kid Astrolabe. But I guess that's . . ." his voice trailed off as he looked guiltily at his brother.

With an elephant in the car so to speak, changing the subject seemed prudent. "What kind of pizza, Hareton? I like vegetarian." Heath, wordlessly, whipped into a parking space near the front of the motel, as I verbally worked my way through Italian sausage, Hawaiian, pepperoni—and stopped as Heath slammed the door and headed toward the motel office.

"I forgot, Jenny. Honest to god, I didn't mean to make Heath think about Sue Ann. I was just trying to win our game and thought of a meaner uncle than Claudius. Heloise's uncle was a vicious old fart. Then I had to go and mention their kid, Astrolabe."

"I wouldn't worry, Hareton. Heath's been a bit strung out the past week. We'll go watch something stupid on TV. Get our minds off things." I couldn't get my mind off things. *The time is out of joint.* I couldn't get Hamlet or his wicked Uncle Claudius out of my mind. Somewhere on the coast of Oregon a blood relative of mine was plying his trade without knowing I existed.

TWO LARGE GREASY pizzas and a liter of coke later, Hareton snored while Heath and I watched Judy Garland's heartstrings going zing-zing-zing until we could no longer bear it.

"*Carpe diem*, Jenny?" Heath eyed my bed and pointed to Hareton sprawled over three-quarters of his queen-sized mattress.

Heath's Latin was situational at best. Suddenly, I remembered that moment in the Zion Chapel when I came upon Josh playing Bach Inventions. Josh had traced a word I used back to its Latin root quite effortlessly.

My elementary French class in Portland had prepared me to find a hotel if I ever traveled to France and conjugate the "er" verbs. The only Latin I could remember was Oregon's state motto.

I flapped my arms wide, taking up the whole of my bed, and said tersely: "*Alis volate proplis*. She flies with her own wings." Then, I flopped over on my stomach and dropped into a troubled sleep.

# CHAPTER 20

The anxiety I was feeling about meeting this ghost of an uncle waned when we hit the 101. Glorious expanses of blue-gray seas splashed around giant haystack rocks along the coast. We parked by the road in Depoe Bay to watch the Coast Guard practicing rescue operations in the most perilous port I could imagine. Cliffs of stone soared high as the boat bounced hither and yon, flirting with disaster.

I thought of the grudge I'd been holding against this absent uncle of mine ever since Mother had flipped her hand toward my father's casket and left the question open-ended about which brother should be under the roses. I had managed to keep the discussion going with myself for months. Solipsistic, Aunt Izzy would say.

Heath and I had clam chowder while Hareton worked his way through a giant platter of fish and chips in Depoe Bay. "Not too far now, Jenny. Florence, Reedsport, Winchester Bay, then we'll be in North Bend and cut over to Charleston."

Like an annoying cartographer, Heath clicked off upcoming towns. "Or, we could stop outside of Reedsport and see the Elk Reserve. Really interesting."

"I'd rather get it over with, Heath. If you and Hareton don't mind." This long-lost uncle search needed to end. I would embrace what happened—either the good or the bad—like a Buddhist. Not the uncle. No embraces there. Standoffish would be my position.

From Depoe Bay to North Bend, foxgloves pushed their feverish spears toward the sun along a dense forest of Douglas fir lining the 101. As Heath turned west toward Charleston, my anxiety had led me to gnaw my fingernails past the obsessive to the clinical.

"It will be OK, Jenny. If you don't like this uncle of yours, we can get the hell out of Dodge." Heath gripped my tortured fingers and smiled over at me. "I can't imagine him not being smitten by you. We all are, you know."

With Heath, I couldn't determine whether his kindness was a form of habitual flirtation with any female or something more serious.

The masts of dozens of boats bobbed in the marina as Heath pulled into a parking space. The crisp salt sea air carried just the hint of fish or crab or something gone off a bit. *Like me*, I thought. *One of those family tree limbs that had been lopped off before it could sprout. Why was I out here on the coast of Oregon looking for an uncle who had not cared enough about family to find out that he had two nieces?* I decided to stay in the car and sulk while Heath and Hareton explored the marina.

"Jenny, I asked that guy down there next to the blue fishing boat if he knew someone named Hal Hatchet." Hareton tugged at my arm as I got out of the car. "The guy said he's down at the end of the jetty walking this way."

His rufous thatch blazed under the afternoon sun. He swaggered down the boardwalk, not belligerently but confidently, as though sidewalks and jetties should be obliged to clear themselves.

He nodded to people on the walkway, cocking his head to the side in a gratuitous manner, shaking off what he didn't want to hear.

Except for a face broiled to a feverish hue, the man walking toward me was, without doubt, James Hatchet, my father. I moved forward to fling myself into his arms and heard only the piercing shout of Hareton before the sun went down.

ROCKING MOTIONS ALWAYS nauseate me. This one wouldn't stop. I could hear soft, indistinct voices around me. Heath was going on and on about the Compound, and Hareton piped up to fill in the empty spaces. The voice asking questions was my father's. And, it wasn't. It was querulous, just this side of snappy. I struggled to sit up, fighting back the bile rising in my throat.

"Stop the rocking," I hissed. "I'm about to . . ."

"Barf bucket, Hareton! Over by the end of the bunk. For charters when a novice sailor can't make it to the side."

With a willfulness that I didn't know I possessed, I pushed my gag reflex down until my only sensation was the fetid taste in my mouth, like milk gone sour, the kind Marybeth used in her puddings. I was determined not to be a novice.

Then, I opened my eyes. I appeared to be inside a boat that continued a persistent rocking. Heath and Hareton knelt beside me. My father's ghost stood beside them watching me with guarded eyes. I mimicked his chary expression and his silence, examining him closely for signs of damage caused by a dunking in the McKenzie River.

This phantom with my father's face wore a thick Arum sweater, the kind that the fishermen's wives in Ireland knit with their own special patterns so they can identify the drowned victim after the fish have nibbled away all the recognizable parts. *From the McKenzie River to the Oregon Coast is not very far. Why had he left us to mourn?*

Guilt was there. I could see it flaring behind those ruddy, sunburned cheeks. The wreck was an excuse for desertion. Mother, Lorena and I had become too much of a burden. I glared up at the man who looked like my father but who wasn't sending out my father's vibes.

"You're not him. You're an impostor." My voice sounded weak, frail with suppressed emotion.

"Not an impostor. An identical twin. Sorry to have frightened you, Jenny. I thought that Clara would have said. The boys told me about James. I'm shocked. I had no idea. No one told me. I would have come."

LAND OF THE BONG TREE

I pushed myself up on the bunk and swung my feet to the floor. This red Esau really didn't look that much like my father with his expression of bewilderment. My father never looked puzzled. If his identical twin brother had died, he would have known.

"What I don't understand is how Clara got hooked up with a bigamist in a religious sect. She was a very particular woman. I guess that's why she dumped me for James." This uncle named Hal tried to smile, but I wasn't the only one tasting bile. He had a mouth full it. I recognized it as lost chances and a bitterness that he still harbored.

"Hooked up is a rude way to describe a kidnapping. Mother, Lorena and I have been kept against our wills behind an electric fence since my birthday. I managed to get away, but they are still captive."

I looked around the inside of the boat. Everything was tidy with a small stove-like affair, one bunk, a couple of chairs and a bank of what appeared to be a sophisticated sound system that Hareton was examining.

"Don't touch the knobs, Hareton!" Heath barked at his brother.

"It's OK. He can't hurt anything. That's my navigation system, Hareton. If you boys have time, I can take you out and show you how it works. You, too, Jenny. If you don't get too seasick."

The pout that I could feel forming on my mouth smoothed out and turned into the most acidic response I could muster against a sudden onset of nausea. "The boys can do what they want to with you. I'll just stay behind and throw up."

With that, I pushed Heath aside, staggered across the floor, climbed up a small ladder and upchucked my lunch of clam chowder to a waiting circle of brown pelicans that didn't seem to object to recycled food. They recycled to their young. Tri-cycled food. I gagged again at the thought.

Standing at the side of the boat and looking into a low-hanging bank of brilliant deep purple clouds to the west, I watched the ocean dimpling with small whitecaps and thought of the allure of all that space beyond with no electric fences.

I strained to make out the words of the voices murmuring below deck. Probably having one of those chinwags about testy females, speculating about "that time of the month." It wasn't that time of the month. It was that time of the moment.

This elusive uncle of mine should have been loading a gun, getting his gear together, setting forth a plan to rescue his sister-in-law and niece from those perverts in the Compound—not discussing a boating trip. I wasn't seasick any longer. I was heartsick.

"Jenny." A slight pat on my shoulder caused an instant reflex away from the calloused hand that touched me. "I wanted to see if you're OK. My house is just a few miles south of here. I think you and your friends will be more comfortable there—until you get your sea legs. You ride with me. Heath and Hareton can follow. Heath is calling his mother to let her know you arrived safely."

# CHAPTER 21

Uncle Hal and I didn't talk during the drive. Well. That's not accurate. I didn't talk. I listened and didn't like everything I heard.

"I was engaged to your mother, to Clara. James went off that summer with a wheat harvesting crew after we graduated from high school. I worked double shifts at restaurants and bars, anywhere that I could get cash. I had planned to study oceanography."

When I glanced over, I noticed that his jaw was rigid. "Oh well. The best laid plans. Clara and her folks had moved to Portland down the street from our house when she was a junior in high school. James and I were seniors and still lived in our parents' house. It was paid for. Our folks died of cancer the year before. Both of them within six months of each other. Heavy smokers. Cured us of that habit."

He ground the gears on a pickup that looked more embattled than that old heap of Josh's. "Clara and I got engaged the summer before she was a senior. Her folks seemed to like me. They asked us to wait for the wedding until she graduated, so we agreed.

Then, I went off to Seattle to start my baccalaureate."

He glanced ruefully over at me. "James came home from wheat harvest with money in his pocket, a nice tan on his face, an absent brother, to Clara."

I turned abruptly to study the flora and fauna. Uncle Hal was making my father appear as an opportunist and my mother as fickle-hearted. Considering how soon Mother left widowhood behind, I could imagine her as a fickle fiancée. But my father was clearly the better twin.

"I don't mean to speak ill of your father, Jenny. We were very close as boys. When I came home between semesters in December, James and Clara had eloped." Uncle Hal—or my father's deserting brother as I chose to think of him— looked at me as though he expected sympathy. I didn't offer so much as a raised eyebrow.

"Clara's parents were furious. So was I. We commiserated together for days. I left on a trawler the next week. When I came back a year later, our parents' house had been sold. My share was in a bank account. I didn't want to see either James or Clara. I bought my own boat, moved to the south coast of Oregon and tried to forget about them."

I know better than to speak without thinking, but how could anyone ever forget about my wonderful, clever father? Or my beautiful, empty-headed mother? "I don't see how you could just close a door to your life. Didn't my father ever try to contact you?"

Uncle Hal flushed. "He did. I'm sorry to have to tell you. The day you were born, he sent me a long letter, asking me to forgive him and Clara for not telling me face to face that they were in love. He asked me to come meet my niece. I read the letter, put it carefully back in the envelope and marked Return to Sender in big letters on the outside."

He pulled his pickup in front of a single-story, white frame house with bright blue wooden shutters. "I don't expect you to understand, Jenny. You're too young. Clara was the most beautiful creature I'd ever seen. She was like a fresh-faced Marilyn Monroe, but unaware of how alluring she could be. I couldn't get her out of my head."

He looked sheepishly over at me. "Then I did. I had lots of friends. Short-lived ones. I got over your mother. I guess I couldn't get past my anger. Now it's too late."

Heath whipped in behind us, and Hareton jumped out to open my door. "Did you see all the seals on those rocks just off the shoreline, Jenny? I've never seen so many in my life. Listen. You can hear them here."

"That might be the traffic off 101. We're just west of it. Get your bags and come in. I have two extra bedrooms." Uncle Hal flung an arm around Hareton's shoulder and immediately began talking about fishing, crabbing and whale watching.

Heath raised one eyebrow, but I answered him with an expressionless face. Not once had my uncle said anything that made me think that he was anything but a grudge-holding Esau. So what if my mother preferred my father? Uncle Hal knew that he had a niece and chose to ignore that fact for fifteen years.

I knew about grudges. I could hold them with the best. My grudge stockpile looked like one of those massive African termite mounds, full of CPRC elders with Marybeth and Mr. Darken capping the top of it.

Swinging my duffle out of the back of Aunt Izzy's car, I followed Uncle Hal inside, thinking I might give him the benefit of the doubt. I looked around the neat house, checking for traces of all those "friends." Not a feminine touch to be seen.

A big stainless gas stove dominated the kitchen. A bank of speakers cluttered one wall of the living room. CDs marched in precision on built-in shelves. Blown-up photographs of giant waves pounding haystack rocks brought the ocean indoors.

The masculine feel of this place comforted me. Mother had affection for whatnots. Elves, glassy-eyed fairies, shepherdesses that appeared to have lost their little woolies were on every available surface of our house—and transmogrified themselves into the apartment after Mother smuggled them out of the yard sale.

Uncle Hal bustled around us as though three unexpected guests might be as routine as the coastal rain. "I'll find something for dinner. You boys take the bedroom on the right. Jenny, in a minute, I'll show you your bedroom."

I liked the way he said "your bedroom," as though I had been a frequent visitor in the past and might be in the future. This uncle of mine could redeem himself, but it would take more than dinner and a free bed.

"I'll defrost some sea bass and throw some potatoes in to bake. I've got a fairly good collection of music, Heath. Just put on what you kids like."

I glowered at Heath. After two hundred miles of Toby Keith and Brad Paisley, I needed to get away from country. It was time to needle this uncle. "You wouldn't happen to have any harpsichord music? Wanda Landowska?" I searched for the esoteric, knowing that someone like Wanda who had recorded seventy-five years ago probably hadn't made it to a record store on the coast.

Uncle Hal took the bait, grinning as though he had just scored highest in Jeopardy. "CDs on the left. They're arranged by genre. I have Landowska playing Handel and Haydn. Maybe Mozart."

So for the next half hour, I listened to the harpsichord and wished I'd asked for Coldplay or Pink Floyd. The soulfully twanging harpsichord unsettled me. Or maybe it was the way that Hareton tagged along with my uncle. Heathcliff sat cross-legged on the floor with a beatific expression as he thumbed through stacks of CDs.

"In this afternoon light with your head turned at that angle, you look exactly like your grandmother, Moira Hatchet. She had your color of hair. It's auburn when the light hits it." He put a big photograph album on the sofa next to me. "This was my mother's. I assume you've seen some of these. James and I divided the photos when our parents died."

I trailed my fingers across the faux leather cover as though I might be stroking the lost jeweled cover of the *Book of Kells*. "I have never seen a single, solitary photograph of the Hatchet family. Mother had one of those garish studio things that had been colored of her parents and tons of photos of her as a girl. Her parents photographed her constantly."

"Her mother was almost past childbearing age when Clara arrived. Their beautiful child overwhelmed them.

They expected to open the door and see Hollywood agents." He frowned. "She couldn't act and refused to memorize anything. That didn't matter to them. They thought she hung the moon."

I eased open the cover of the photo album. The redheaded twins stood between two proud parents whose cigarettes dangled like Bogart and Bacall. Uncle Hal sat down next to me, uncomfortably close, and pointed out his grandparents, sober in a sepia print. "Irish immigrants. Their parents before them came from County Cork. My grandfather was a fisherman on the Oregon Coast. I guess it's in my genes."

A loud snap and a spray of sparks sent Uncle Hal flying off the sofa to stare in dismay at a limp plastic plug, melting like one of Dali's watches. "Damn and blast! I knew that was going to happen. Getting an electrician to come out when I can be here is nigh on to impossible."

"Jenny's one." Hareton piped up. "She fixed Mom's old fuzzy lamp plugs and replaced a wall socket in the kitchen. She would have electrocuted those geeks in the Compound, but someone caught her."

"You've overloaded your circuit. You have a first-rate sound system and 1940s electrical wiring. I saw the problem the minute we walked into the door. It's a wonder you haven't torched your house with all those extension cords hooked together. I've seen worse. The Zion Chapel in the Compound. I fixed that to my satisfaction," I said primly as though I was the judge and jury for anything with a current.

Uncle Hal sunk to the couch and put his head between his hands. Hareton patted his back abstractly as though he couldn't understand how a few sparks could distress this man of the sea.

"You sounded just like your father then, Jenny. For a moment, just thinking about James made me sad. He was the ultimate tinkerer, put together little motors for our toys from scratch. Loved math. His pastime was repairing the old clocks. He bought them at junk shops and sold them to antique stores. He was saving money to study math in college. Did he?"

"Did he what?" I knew what Uncle Hal was asking, but I didn't want to talk about failed dreams.

"Get a baccalaureate in mathematics? Finish college? Work in that field?" Uncle Hal's questions had taken on an urgency that made me uncomfortable. I needed to set up a detour before he got any closer to the truth of missed opportunity.

"We studied Euclid together. He helped me with my homework. Because of him, I was the best math student in my class. I've done some trig and was ready to start on calculus when . . ." My words dropped off abruptly, and I flipped frantically through the pages of my grandmother's photo album, searching for something, anything.

"When what?" Uncle Hal put his fingers on my chin and turned my face toward him.

The questions behind his hooded eyes held unfathomable pain. At the moment, I felt mean-spirited enough to cause him more. My father always told me that he'd go to college after "his girls had finished school," but I knew that wasn't true, not after Mother had charged her first pair of Manolo Blahniks. She was lining the racks in her closest faster than Carrie Bradshaw.

"When what?" Uncle Hal repeated again.

"When he drove a semi into the McKenzie River, and the life we had disappeared." There. Right between the eyes. The expression on his face took on a new level of puzzlement.

"Didn't you stay in the same school? Your house? Surely James . . ." Now Uncle Hal's words were dropping off.

"The company he was driving for said that he wasn't a regular employee, just a temporary. Their insurance didn't cover him." That fact put the onus on that crummy company. I didn't want to talk about Mother's purchase of a coffin fit for a Tudor king or a stone that stood six feet tall or maxed-out credit cards.

I switched the subject. "I didn't know I had an uncle until Mother mentioned it just as they were lowering . . . not lowering . . . waiting to . . . and you didn't . . ." All I could remember of that dreadful day was a vicious slash in the ground and a layer of ugly artificial grass—the color of green that pours out of steers after they've been on winter wheat.

Now, Uncle Hal changed the subject, popping off the sofa faster than a jack-in-the-box. "Dinner's almost ready. Hareton, will you grab some plates? Heath, can you flip the fish on the grill out back? I got absorbed by the past and forgot that you kids must be starving."

Uncle Hal's backyard bloomed with rhododendrons as high as his house with sheaves of pink and purple splaying out over the grass. The setting would be perfect for one of those glamorous weddings where nobody notices that the flowers alone cost more than most people earn in a year.

"They grow wild here," Uncle Hal said dismissively as though rhododendrons might have been noxious weeds. "Check out the ocean view." He waved an arm expansively as though beckoning it forward.

Under a dome of fearless blue, untaxed by a single cloud, the sea rolled velvety gray, a troubled shade for such a bright, unhampered day.

"What about tsunamis? I saw warning signs all along the 101." Hareton was less interested in flowers and scenic views than disasters.

"They say the plates just off the coast are gearing up for something one of these days, but the last really big one was centuries ago. The Japanese kept good records. The sirens went off for hours the morning that one hit Japan recently, but we didn't get so much as a wave. Some of the debris is washing up though. Could bring invasive creatures." Uncle Hal smiled across at Hareton's eager face.

"Not like E.T. Or the monster from the Black Lagoon. Crustaceans that are not native to these waters might damage our own species."

THE NATIVE SEA bass was divine, almost as good as my salmon. Not quite, but almost. The view, the salt air, and the perfume of flowers created a sumptuous setting, but the rust was a bit off putting. Two of the three legs of Uncle Hal's grill were swathed in duct tape. His metal chairs left streaks of reddish powder on my backside.

Neither Hareton nor Heathcliff seemed to notice. They were mesmerized by stories of toothy sharks and unexpected gales. I yawned rudely to shift the attention to me. I wasn't ready to end the discussion we seemed to be avoiding.

Uncle Hal stayed in the limelight. "I've got an idea!" He boomed out just as we had polished off a half-gallon of chocolate chip ice cream. "The crabs are so thick they're practically climbing up onto the docks. We can get licenses for you three tomorrow and head up the river. The water won't be rough, Jenny. You'll have fun."

I wasn't sure that I was destined to have fun again, not until I had my mother and sister away from those CPRC deviants. I'd only eaten Dungeness crab once. Too expensive. "Too much trouble," Mother proclaimed, preferring mac and cheese in a box for 79 cents and only one pan to wash.

The bedroom that Uncle Hal showed me was startling, not at all consistent with his masculine style of décor in the rest of the house. Great swoops of dimity curtains hung alongside a bank of windows looking toward the sea. A luscious emerald green satin comforter covered the bed. On the wall was an enlarged photo of the same woman I'd seen in the album, my grandmother, Moira Hatchet.

"Just because I never contacted your parents or you, Jenny, didn't mean that I don't think of you. When I bought this house a few years ago, I thought that this room would be perfect for my niece if she ever came to visit. I even put up your grandmother's photo."

His sigh seemed to take the air out of the room. "Little did I dream that you'd be a dead ringer for your grandmother. Right down to the color of your hair."

There was something eerie about standing in this room with a grandmother I'd never seen staring at me out of my eyes. I couldn't understand why my father had never talked about his parents. I could understand why he was at odds with his brother. Guilt, I suppose.

Then I remembered something. In fourth grade, we were told to write our own autobiographies and illustrate them with photos. When I asked Mother about photos of my father's family, she seemed flustered. "The movers lost the box with James's old papers and books. Just junk from his parents' house. He was so upset with me because I forgot to tell him it was missing. Until it was too late. They couldn't find it. Such a fuss he made over old junk, old photos. Worst quarrel we ever had."

Uncle Hal waited in the doorway as though he expected me to comment. I never disappoint. "If you want to see a dead ringer for someone, you should meet your other niece, Lorena. She's seven. And, a dead ringer for Mother right down to the roots of her blond hair." With that, I closed the door, whipped back the comforter and fell into bed fully clothed.

# CHAPTER 22

Crabbing is everything its cracked up to be, if you don't mind the slimy turkey legs that lure the crabs to their death or the back-breaking weight of tossing traps overboard without hitting the boat and dragging them back crawling with frantic crabs.

A brisk wind kept the boat drifting away from the shoreline. In spite of a blazing sun that caused Heath and Hareton to dump their life vests and shirts, I buckled my vest like a whalebone corset about me. Uncle Hal didn't need to know that I couldn't swim a stroke. He did give me sound advice about picking an unmovable spot on the horizon and staying focused whenever I felt queasy.

"You're strong for a girl, Jenny." He intended to compliment me, I suppose, but it was backhanded at best.

Before I could think of a response, Heathcliff chimed in. "You should see her run, Mr. Hatchet. She's a 10K runner, fast as a bolt of lightening. Doesn't run like any girl I've ever known."

My stock was rising. I would send it higher. "I made a list of the things you'll need for me to fix your electrical problems at the house. I assume you have tools there?"

"You're my guest, Jenny. You don't have to work. I'll get an electrician over next week."

I suspected that Uncle Hal couldn't believe that a girl could possibly do electrical work to his satisfaction—though his standards appeared to be very low, considering the number of extension cords humping each other like rabbits.

"Payment for the crabbing and for putting us up. Actually, I like doing it. Clears the head wonderfully." I tossed off his rejection blithely.

"Then take the wheel of the boat. That really clears the head. I've cured hangovers with nothing but sea air and the feel of a wheel in my hands." He gave the wheel a pat and walked away.

"But I don't know how . . . I never have . . ." The boat seemed to be drifting dangerously near a giant stack of black rocks, just at the point where the river churned violently. I grabbed the wheel and jerked. The boat spun halfway around.

"Easy does it, Jenny. You can feel the movement of the river right up through the wheel. Don't fight it. Just go with it." The look on Uncle Hal's face might have suggested a moment of fear, but he never moved away from dragging in the crabs, tossing back the females, and measuring the males.

By early afternoon, we had our quota and headed for the cleaning station further up the river. That was the disgusting part. Avoiding those lethal pincers and whacking the belly-up crabs while their claws beat the air helplessly was almost more than I could bear.

The bile was rising again.

"You're so pale that your freckles are showing, Jenny," Hareton crowed as he scooped out crab innards and tossed them to the waiting gulls. "Midair this time! Good catch, bird."

"Take a walk, Jenny. We'll be done here in fifteen minutes. Hareton really has the rhythm of cleaning crab down pat. You got too much sun this morning. I forgot that you kids live in a forest. Too much sun can make you ill."

Happily, Uncle Hal was blaming my nausea on Donne's "busy old fool unruly sun." Just watching the gutting and cleaning of crabs stirred up my queasiness worse than a rocking boat. I wandered down the dock, far away from the odor of fish and watched Hareton, Heathcliff and Uncle Hal. There was a kind of grace to their crab-cleaning ballet as they moved in tandem—whack, scoop, wash, and layer on ice.

THE CRABS BOILING in a stainless steel pot in the backyard were odorless, their small slivers of pearly flesh delicious beyond compare. I mastered the art of cracking shells, teasing out the meat, and dipping it into melted butter with the appetite of someone who has just survived the Bataan march.

"Try some garlic bread and coleslaw, Jenny. Crab can be a bit rich if you're not used to it."

I pushed back my chair and my plate at the same time. I wasn't used to anything rich like expensive crab. I had become accustomed to that shabby apartment we had to move to in Portland—never could feel at home in that harem of Mr. Darken's.

Before Josh had dumped me on the mercy of the Earnshaws, I had been a captive in an attic—not a handsome, stone turret like the one where Mr. Rochester kept his mad wife, just a poorly furnished attic made into a bedroom for a guest who didn't want to be there.

Jerry Winner breathing hoarsely outside the door with a bulge in his pants would have sent me rappelling fearlessly over the edge of the Grand Canyon if I hadn't finally managed to scale three stories with the paracord that Josh's mother sneaked past the Winner wives.

Riches beyond imagination blessed the Earnshaw house—not just the Native American collection of art in every room. The spirit of love that the Earnshaws demonstrated for each member of their family—and for me, the outsider—swept over me with the force of a spring breeze as I stared across that endless ocean toward the west.

It was time to go back. To leave this place. I had spent enough time with Uncle Hal to know that the love of his life was the water, his boat, and his solitary existence. I had no right to interfere with it. He had chosen to absent himself from our family by nurturing a grudge against my father and mother. So what if it kept him from ever knowing that little charmer Lorena?

She belonged to me. So did Mother and her shoe fetish. Someday, I'd make enough money to buy her all the red-soled shoes her feet could desire. In the meantime, I had to get her out of jail—before Mr. Darken, using some kind of cult psychology, managed to convince her that she loved her captors. It happened to Patty Hearst, and she probably had more Jimmy Choos than Mother could imagine.

IF I EXPECTED consolation from Heathcliff or sympathy from Hareton, I was barking up the wrong tree. "I think it is a really creepy thing to do, leaving like this at night. Mr. Hatchett has been really nice to us, Jenny. He had to go fill up his boat, but he'll be back within the hour. He said so." Hareton's voice soared up and down like a frustrated diva searching for her range.

I tried to explain as I stuffed my duffle in the back of Aunt Izzy's Honda. "Yeah. He's been nice to us. Very hospitable. What he hasn't been is helpful. Not once did he suggest that he would help us get Mother and Lorena out of the Compound. Not once!" I barked at Hareton and was instantly sorry when I saw his chin tremble. Maybe his brother would understand.

"Things are heating up at the Compound, Heath. The treatment of Josh and his mother is bizarre. If the elders try to make her marry Elder Grund, you know that Josh will do something desperate. You saw the men with their Uzis. That wasn't happening before I left. They were buying guns. I knew that. I looked in Mr. Darken's off-limits basement room. But, they weren't patrolling with them every day."

I tugged on Heath's arm. "Maybe they got wind of something. A raid from the Feds, like the one in Texas with the Branch Davidians. We must get home. I have a bad feeling. We need to go without any delay. I left a note for my uncle, thanking him for his hospitality. We're done here." I shoved Hareton into the back seat, climbed into the passenger's seat and waited for Heath to turn the key.

"I think we're being very rude not to wait for your uncle. He might decide to help. You don't really know, Jenny." Heath turned the key and backed slowly out of the yard.

"He knows the problem. He didn't make a single comment about how he might assist—other than to tell me that Mother's marriage to a bigamist isn't legal. I know that! Drive, Heath. Go." I could hear Hareton sniveling in the backseat. Uncle Hal had promised to show him how to use the navigation system on the boat. He might not forgive me today. He would tomorrow. He was that kind of sweet-tempered boy.

BY THE TIME we got to a seedy motel in Eugene, Heath's temper flared. "Mother said to stay in a nice motel. She gave me cash to cover it. We're likely to get bedbugs in this joint." He looked at the saggy mattresses and stained carpet.

The motel looked more like our apartment in Portland than I'd ever admit, right down to the mold darkening the spaces between the floor tiles in the bathroom. If, by any chance, Uncle Hal came searching for us, he wouldn't look in a fleabag motel. "I read that bedbugs are invading five-star hotels now, so it's pretty much a crapshoot these days."

"*Les jeux sont faits!*" Heath grinned at me and plopped down on the bed with the best view of the TV. He could occasionally surprise me with his fatalistic comment that the chips are down. But Jean-Paul Sartre was a step up from his recent fixation on Henry Bukowski in my opinion.

I rolled up a slightly soiled comforter and inspected the sheets. One of my friends had told me her mother and aunt cleaned motel rooms. They could do it in half the time if they didn't change the sheets—they just stood across from each other, popped up the used sheets to get rid of errant hairs, and smoothly tucked them in.

Some people had probably never slept on a sheet. We were spoiled to the good life, but considering the yellowish hue of the sheets, I kept on my clothes and propped myself up while Heath flipped through a stingy assortment of channels.

# CHAPTER 23

By time we were heading up Highway 101 the next morning after swinging through the Golden Arches, Hareton's good humor had returned. "I'll bet Dad has never been crabbing. He's probably never had crabs."

"I hope not," Heath interjected while I maintained an impassive face.

"We can go back, Jenny. Anytime. Mr. Hatchet told me on the boat that we were always welcome at his house—and on his boat. He said he'd take me deep-sea fishing if Mom didn't object. When do you think we could go back?"

Hareton's pleading unsettled me—as though I had left something unfinished behind. I had no answer for him.

Heath passed his prized iPod and earphones over the backseat to his brother. "Don't figure out a way to break this, or you'll never hear the last of it from me."

"We need to talk, Jenny. I'm not so sure that your uncle wouldn't have helped us. He seems like a nice guy. When you mistook him for your father and passed out on that dock in front of everyone, he scooped you up so fast it made my head spin. He was shocked too. He didn't know his brother had died or his sister-in-law had taken up . . . I mean been taken by a pervert."

That little slip might have released the stream of invective that had been curling around my tongue ever since I realized we'd made this trip in vain. My long-lost uncle wasn't going to help us. I glared at Heath.

"Given the fact that you didn't want to give him a chance to redeem himself by waiting just a few more hours puts the problem back in our camp." Heath touched my arm lightly, as though he knew it was brittle as glass— and cold as ice.

"We use logic. That's what we do. That means we figure out the weaknesses of our opponents and go after those." I said reasonably but without a single strategy in mind.

"We're not facing Napoleon's army or the Spanish Armada, Jenny. Our enemies have lived in this area all of their lives. I can't imagine how far their network stretches. Josh's father told Dad about his concern that some of the elders were becoming much more radical. That's why he had planned to take his family and leave. You know where that idea got him."

I had never seen a picture of Josh's dad, but I could imagine a mild-mannered CPA who played Bach Inventions on the piano squaring off against a mad bull. It wasn't an image I wanted to dwell on.

"Here's the thing. Lorena is underage—you are too, even though you could pass for twenty." Heath winked at me. I knew he was trying to lighten the conversation after bringing up Josh's unfortunate father and that bull.

"Your mother is your legal guardian unless the state steps in for some reason. From what you've told me, Mr. Darken is using psychological torture—separating her from Lorena—and using drugs like Valium to keep her in line."

"Aren't those crimes? Kidnapping a child from her mother? Forcing her to take drugs that can only be prescribed by a doctor? Shouldn't the police simply act on that information alone?"

"Nothing simple about it, Jenny. The Compound is private property. Even if official channels worked, and we could get a search warrant, somebody in the sheriff's office or someone on the Res would tip off the elders. By the time any officials got inside, your mother would be threatened into silence, and Lorena would be off visiting a non-existent relative, nowhere to be found."

Heath flung one arm across the back of my seat and fiddled with my French braid—my solution to unwashed hair. "Gramps is doing work behind the scenes, visiting with some key members on the Tribal Council. He has to be careful that Ebon Riley doesn't get wind of anything. Ebon is thick as thieves with Darken and some of the elders in the Compound."

I watched Heath's lips reshape themselves into a thin, bitter line. I knew that he was thinking about someone else with whom Ebon might have been "thick as thieves." I needed to help him think about anything but Sue Ann's broken body curled up on the forest thatch for a last sleep.

"You really believe what you said last night—*les jeux sont faits*?" I grimaced at my own stupidity. Unanswerable philosophical questions could hardly change the subject from Sue Ann's death.

"I was just showing off my elementary French," Heath answered blithely, then turned a serious face to me. "The dice are cast. No more bets. What's going to happen is already cast in stone. Do I believe that?"

I nodded. "I read that play by Sartre. Eve and Pierre get a chance to relive their lives so that they can fulfill their fate to be together. They know what is supposed to happen, but they can't make it happen. I don't appreciate Sartre," I said grimly. "I have to believe that I can help make things turn out better."

Heath stared straight ahead as we zipped along just slightly over the speed limit, and then announced: "Back to your idea about figuring out your opponent's weaknesses. I told you I did some boxing in high school. Not Mom's idea of a good sport. I learned a strategy that you and your old friend Euclid would appreciate. You pivot and step to the side to create an angle. That creates an advantage for you over your opponent."

"I don't see how a boxing strategy has anything to do with getting Mother and Lorena away from those perverts." I'd rarely talked to a boy who didn't love making sports analogies. Tiresome.

"Side-stepping. Creating a little diversion. That's what I'm talking about. I don't know how we can legally get your family away—or help Josh and his mother. But, if that fence has some weak places as you claimed, we might get some help from . . ." His voice trailed off as he sped around a pickup with a menacing load of trash.

"It's illegal!" His sharp words woke Hareton who leaned over the seat, rubbing his eyes, shell-shocked by miles of heavy metal in his ears.

"The little diversion you were considering or that overloaded truck?" I responded.

"Both." His smile was wicked. I liked it. For the first time since we had fled my uncle's house in Charleston, I felt as though the table were still open. Bets were possible. I would bet on Heathcliff and Gramps.

BATHROOM STOPS WHEN we filled up the car and odd forms of fast food—strawberry twisters, caffeine-loaded energy drinks, and corn dogs that appeared to have suffered a slow death in the fryer—kept us churning on down the road past Portland and angling toward Spokane.

By late afternoon, we were taking what Heath called a "shortcut" through Spokane neighborhoods. It brought to mind the last shortcut we took on our run through gardens and backyards on the Res. It led us to the lake road and Sue Ann's shattered body. Heath's shortcuts made me nervous.

So did Hareton stuffing one earplug into my head. "Black Sabbath! Before Ozzie left. Listen to 'Bark at the Moon.' Man. I love it."

"Vengeance is boiling" cranked up to the max on Heath's iPod shattered my tympanic membrane. "Not really my kind of music, Hareton. And I have a fondness for bats. They are critical to the ecosystem."

Hareton sank back, obviously miffed at me, so I partially redeemed myself. "I love Pink Floyd. And Coldplay." Then, I could say no more. Just mentioning Coldplay took me back to that day I spent with Josh down in the canyon. The picnic. The music. Just thinking about being in the cab of his old pickup with him brought my knees together involuntarily.

"Stop! Stop! The Farmer's Market is today. Right over there. We need to get something for Mom. She likes that home-baked stuff." Hareton's shout brought me back to the present—and a scene that sent chills down my spine.

Not ten feet away from the car stood Marybeth Darken with Leah Winner at the corner of a makeshift stand that had a banner proclaiming "Organically Fresh" above it.

I could see jars of last year's blackberry jam and boxes with pink ribbon trying to disguise the lye soap branded as Scion Soap. Stacks of Mrs. Barnes's lovely sea green pottery lined the base of the stand like an afterthought. She was nowhere to be seen.

Venal right down to the ends of their grasping fingers, Leah Winner and Marybeth Darken were holding up swollen loaves of bread to passersby, proclaiming the bread to be totally organic—whatever that meant. Pesticides and herbicides filled the sheds in the Compound.

Heathcliff didn't appear to recognize them. He probably wouldn't. Only the men came to the Res on business—not the women. He backed expertly into a small space just down the street. "Let's go look around. I need to stretch my legs."

"You and Hareton go. I'm a bit tired. Don't forget that Aunt Izzy likes wheat bread with sunflower and flax seeds. Maybe try that stand over there." I pointed to one halfway down the block. "The one we just passed doesn't look clean." I flipped my thumb toward the CPRC booth with its organically fresh banner waving in the afternoon breeze.

Marybeth would sizzle at my remark. Vinegar and bleach were her bosom companions. Heath cast me a puzzled glance. "I thought you might like to look around a bit. They have everything from handmade jewelry to cheap sunglasses here. It's fun to look."

"I'll come find you and Hareton in a bit." I waved them away and sunk down in my seat so that the CPRC women couldn't see me.

Shaking uncontrollably, I peered through the back-seat window. Another woman stood behind the booth to the far right side. Maylene Darken. She had brought the aspidistra plant to my attic room as a gift from Josh's mother, a gift in a tightly woven macramé holder with just enough paracord to let me escape down three stories. And a pocketknife buried in the roots of the plant.

Maybe Maylene was just an unwitting accomplice. She didn't seem overly bright with all her versifying. But her last whisper—before Leah Winner bullied her out of my attic room—was one of reassurance. I needed to see her. Just her. Not the others.

Bright blue portable toilets crouched like after-thoughts to good hygiene across the market square. Maylene whipped out of the stand, said something to Marybeth, flung her hand in that direction, and headed toward the porta-potties.

I scooted over to the driver's side, eased the door open, slid out, and took flight. By cutting over to the adjacent street and circling the far side of the market, I reached the back of the smelly blue toilets and waited.

Maylene's gasp when she came out might have been the result of her holding her breath inside or the sight of a Compound escapee.

"Jenny! What are you doing here?" She clutched my arm and glanced frantically around us. "It isn't safe. Jerry and Enoch brought us over here today. They could be anywhere."

She swiveled her head in both directions, grabbed my arm in a vise-like grip, thrust me back behind the toilets, and pulled me down into a squatting position.

It was a very strange moment, hunkered down com-panionably behind privies with Maylene stroking the side of my face—as though we weren't on view from 180 degrees where three streets intersected. She said, "Jenny, you're back. Jenny, you're back," like a distressed parrot.

"Just passing through, Maylene. Not back." I gingerly pried her fingers loose only to find them clamping tighter. I tried a diversion. "I saw Marybeth and Leah back there at your booth. Then, I noticed you heading toward the toilets. I didn't mean to startle you." I looked over her shoulder at the intersection full of people. "Can we talk somewhere else, Maylene? I don't think these things have been dumped for a decade." Seasickness was nothing to the nausea overwhelming me at the moment.

"There. Over there. Between those two buildings. See that alley blocked off? There's no traffic there. I'll go first. You follow me." I headed off at a fast clip without looking back as though certain that Maylene would oblige me. It was a gamble, but we were too visible, even crouched behind the toilets.

In the narrow, dim alley, brick walls soared into a sky that had lost its color.

So had Maylene's face. All the buttermilk baths in the world couldn't hide the splotches of freckles that popped out of her ashen cheeks.

"Don't worry, Maylene. You won't get into trouble. No one can see us here. I just need to know about Mother and Lorena. You can't imagine how worried I've been. Are they all right?"

"Right as rain, wouldn't you say, Enoch?"

The calloused thumbs violating my neck probed savagely for the sweet spot on my carotid. I didn't need Hareton's iPod in my ear to hear Ozzy Osborne in my head as I tumbled into darkness with the next line of the song splintering both eardrums: "He's returned to kill the life."

*End of Book Two of the Land Trilogy*

# THE LAND TRILOGY

*Land of Nod*

*Land of the Bong Tree*

*Land of Lyonesse*

Coming soon! *Land of Lyonesse* is the third novel in the *Land Trilogy* featuring Jenny Hatchet.

# Land of Lyonesse

### Charleston, Oregon

**Hal Hatchet:** After my identical twin James eloped with my fiancée Clara seventeen years ago, I removed the word "regret" from my lexicon. Yesterday, I was broadsided by regret when the mirror image of my long-dead mother wearing a mini skirt came strutting down the boardwalk at the Charleston marina and passed out at my feet.

I had never seen my fifteen-year-old niece, Jenny Hatchet, nor did I know that my twin brother had died over a year ago driving a truck into the McKenzie River. My shock when a teenage girl collapsed at my feet couldn't compare to the thunderbolt that struck Jenny who thought she was seeing her father back from the grave.

The fickleness of her mother Clara—who had unknowingly married a polygamist two months ago and taken both of her daughters off to a remote compound in Idaho— didn't surprise me in the least. Jenny had escaped from the perverts to a nearby Native American reservation, but Clara and her younger daughter remained as captives in the compound.

This beautiful, bright, but resentful niece of mine appeared out of nowhere with two boys, Heathcliff and Hareton, from the family who had sheltered her on the nearby reservation. So, in a state of disbelief about what had happened to my brother's family, I tried to make amends to Jenny. I guess I didn't try hard enough. I should have instantly called out the National Guard or taken my rifle and laid siege to the polygamy compound.

After the happiest day I can remember in years of being on the river and crabbing with my niece and her two friends, they disappeared. The boys had been ecstatic about my plans for an ocean fishing trip the next day. When I left to gas up the boat, I returned to find them gone and a perfunctory thank-you note from Jenny.

The brevity, terseness, and underlying criticism in her note cut me to the quick: "Dear Uncle Hal, Thank you for your hospitality. I will manage to rescue Mother and Lorena without your help. Have a nice life catching fish. Jenny."

# CHAPTER 1

Stuffed into a coffin-shaped box in Jerry Winner's van, the only part of my stiffening carcass still functioning was my brain.

When Jerry's crusty thumbs circled my neck today in that alley in Spokane, I could feel him palpating my sternocleidomastoid muscle, searching for the dead giveaway of a throbbing fountain near the fourth cervical vertebra.

Bingo. Contact. Blackness. I would go to my grave with an image of Munch's screamer imprinted on my retinas. The scream came from the gaping mouth of Maylene Darken, one of the two stepmothers that my mother's bigamist husband, Gomer Obadiah Darken, had foisted off on me.

When Heathcliff Earnshaw, his younger brother Hareton, and I stopped by the Farmers Market in Spokane—after our pointless trip to the Oregon Coast to find my missing uncle and get his help—I had lured Maylene into an alley for a chinwag about the status of my mother and little sister.

Like a candy-ass, I'd left my mother and sister Lorena behind when I escaped from the Compound of Perversion, better known as the Church of the Protectors of Restored Christianity in Northern Idaho.

Minutes ago, death had paid me a visit via Jerry's thumbs. Of that I was certain. Ever since the sudden death of my father, who veered his truck into the McKenzie River, I sensed that the old hooded spook with the scythe was just waiting for the right moment to whack me.

Flat on my back in a makeshift casket, I could feel every bump in the road. The disgusting odor of lye infused with thyme let me know that the bulges alongside my neck were bars of unsold soap from the Farmers Market. I was sharing my coffin with leftover "organic" products that rankled with pesticides and chemicals.

All that postmortem speculation about lights at the end of the tunnel could be put to rest. I could feel an opaque glaze gelling under my closed lids. Organs with no oxygen did whatever they did with no more bodily functions to support. They went flaccid as an old dishrag.

The soup making of putrefaction must already be underway in my body—all those anaerobic organisms proliferating faster than Sherman marched through Atlanta. Give me three to six hours, and my limbs would be as rigid as flagpoles. Another few hours and bloat from methane would turn me into a puffer fish.

Without an undertaker's palette of makeup, my face would discolor into a bluish-purple that wouldn't go well with my chestnut hair. Vanity seemed to be traveling into the grave with me.

It's probably not a light at the end of the tunnel that the newly revived recall; it's most likely the victim's last cognizant struggle to preserve the brain against microbes fighting their way up to the big valve, the one where Jerry put his odious thumb.

I tried to remember the Bouthillier nomenclature but couldn't get past cervical, petrous, and lacerum as I worked my way mentally up the vertebrae of my neck, wondering where the blood stopped pumping.

When the old van chugged through the Compound gates, I could envision the reception my corpse would get. Jerry Winner and Enoch Bonner might bear me through the gates on their shoulders like the fallen queen Boudicca who chose death over captivity.

Or, they might not. They might just plop me into that murky pond where Jerry dumped my friend Abigail Johnson.

Dismal thoughts shouldn't torment the last moments of the dead, but I was in mental throes over being dumped into water more than six inches deep. Can't swim. Even a bathtub of water can send my blood pressure soaring.

If those Uzi-toting elders let the van into the Compound, I reflected, with a tinge of satisfaction, that some of the CPRCers might faintly regret their treatment of me, especially after I'd rewired their soap factory and chapel.

I might have descended into blindness, but I could still imagine Mother and my little sister wailing over my limp body; I visualized their future. Mother would sink into a Valium fog. Lorena would be tutored in obedience until one of those Abraham-demented men decided a thirteen-year-old nubile girl was age-appropriate for the sacrificial altar of a "celestial marriage."

Maybe a marriage with our own stepfather, Gomer Darken. I had watched him holding Lorena on his lap, nuzzling her tousled golden locks like a hog rooting for truffles, smirking at Mother as though he had just found Lolita.

The van hit a big pothole, jarring my backbone like a string of off-centered dominoes. I had a sudden vision of myself as Lazarus from a Fifteenth Century Byzantine icon, standing with a halo glinting around my head while peasants picked at my mummy wrappings.

I stirred. From my dead toes to somewhere in the recesses of my tortured brain, things were moving. From beyond the veil—or whatever dark place I had gone—I squeezed my eyes open just a slit to see a tunnel of light. It was coming through a very dirty back window of Jerry's van.

At that moment, Emily Dickinson breathed her poem about hope into my deaf ears.

*Hope is the thing with feathers*
*That perches in the soul*
*And sings the tune*
*Without the words*
*and never stops at all.*

I flung myself into an upright position so quickly that my head gyrated, scrambling the light like a lopsided kaleidoscope. Pottery plates flew in all directions; bars of

Sion soap skidded across the ridged metal floor, and I stared into the shocked faces of three women sitting on wooden benches along the side of the van as though they were being transported to lockdown.

The llama face of Marybeth Darken, stepmother number two, looked primed for a good spit. Maylene, stepmother number one, had the grace to utter words that the other two women would never speak: "Praise the Lord. She's restored."

*And with all her wits about her* I wanted to scream to high heaven into those disbelieving faces.

Another novel by **Peggy Gardner**

# A WINDING SHEET

The dark and twisted past of her ancestor, Octavius Wolfe, ensnares his only living descendant in a web of century-old murders as Isabella Wolfe, a young physician, returns to her ancestral home in Southern Oklahoma.

*A Winding Sheet* entangles Isabella in a past that will not be denied in spite of her self-imposed exile for fifteen years. Desperate to discover the link between recent deaths and the hundred-year-old bones of two young girls in her family cemetery, Isabella challenges an instrument of death that hangs by her own family tree.

*A Winding Sheet* takes Isabella into a sinister world where her great-great grandfather's dream of an empire threatens the life of his only living descendant.

What reviewers are saying about *A Winding Sheet:*

"I was hoping the story would never end, because it was so beautifully written, just like a song that you could listen to over and over again."

—E. F.


"A thoroughly enjoyable, superbly crafted book. An enthralling novel with an authentic sense of the stark atmosphere of Southern Oklahoma."

—G. H.


Gardner's lush, evocative descriptions of the Oklahoma landscape are those of a writer lovingly familiar with her subject, her keen medical insight that of an observant insider. This masterfully crafted and detailed novel will have you on the edge of your seat."

—J. M.

# ACKNOWLEDGMENTS

Many thanks to my friends and relatives who have read *Land of the Bong Tree* and suggested improvements, especially the Bandon Writers Group.

I am indebted to Debbie O'Byrne for her striking cover design.

# ABOUT THE AUTHOR

Peggy Gardner began her career as a journalist, taught English Literature, managed medical education, clinics and research for a major hospital, and has traveled extensively with her husband, daughter, and son. She currently resides in Oregon for the incomparable splendor of its coast.

Proof

Made in the USA
Charleston, SC
19 February 2016